ESCAPE TO
HONG KONG

ESCAPE TO
HONG KONG

Audrey Constant

CHRISTIAN FOCUS PUBLICATIONS

©1994 Christian Focus Publications
ISBN 1 85792 063 5

Published by
Christian Focus Publications
Geanies House, Fearn, Tain, Ross-shire
IV20 1TW, Scotland, Great Britain

Cover design by Donna Macleod
Cover illustration by Joan Corlass

Printed and bound in Great Britain by
Cox & Wyman Ltd, Reading, Berks

CONTENTS

Chapter 1

Dusk was settling over the sea when Trang spotted the island, the first sight of land in three weeks. A stiff breeze drove the boat over the crested waves and into the shelter of the cove. As it touched shore, Trang stepped out onto firm sand.

He was surprised to find how weak he was. He had difficulty in standing upright and even when Banh came to lend a hand with the boat, it was all they could do to drag it in. They pulled down the mainsail which was now so tattered as to be almost useless. The jib had long since gone, having been ripped from its stays in a storm.

'That will do for now,' said Trang. 'We'll tie the rope round this tree.' He pointed to where a young fir had managed to take root between the rocks. As the son of a fisherman he knew how to handle boats and now he looped the rope round the trunk and secured it.

He glanced at his sister. Mimi lay in the bottom of the boat, her head on his jacket. Her eyes were closed and she looked so frail that Trang feared that she might die before they could get help for her. She had had nothing to eat or drink for days, not since they finished the small amount of food and water left by the pirates.

'This can't be Hong Kong?' said Banh, looking about the small rocky island. At eighteen he was a year older than Trang and heavily built whereas Trang was light boned and when fit, strong and quick on his feet. Like all Vietnamese, they both had somewhat flattish features with black hair and dark brown eyes.

It was to Trang that the refugees had looked when it came to making decisions, one of the reasons being that the boat in which they had made their escape belonged to his father. Since South Vietnam had been overrun by the Northern Communists, the people had been fleeing from persecution, escaping in any way they could in search of a better life. Most of them had left in boats and although some survived, many had died in the attempt. But still they continued to leave.

Trang's father had prepared him well for the voyage, poring over maps and weather charts. Trang had studied them so carefully that he knew most of them by heart. It was just as well, because one day the wind took hold of the well worn map and whipped it from his hands, carrying it a long way before it finally settled on the sea.

'I reckon Hong Kong can't be far away,' said Trang. 'If we're where I think we are there are hundreds of these islands scattered about. Some of them belong to Hong Kong but others are owned by Communist China.'

'Do you think they're inhabited?' asked Banh.

'Certainly some of the bigger ones are and probably a few fishermen live on the smaller ones,' said Trang.

He thought Hong Kong must be somewhere to the west, though without the map, he couldn't be sure. He looked around. Behind the rocky shore, wooded slopes rose to a bare rugged peak. Trang could see other islands in the distance, but not a boat in sight.

'Looks as though we shall have to stay here till someone comes and rescues us. There must be fishermen in the area,' said Banh.

'If we're near Hong Kong, the police will be patrolling the waters as well,' said Trang. 'We'll have to steer clear of them.' His father had warned him about that. 'But we've got to get help for Mimi.'

'Then we shall have to take risks,' said Banh. 'At least we'll find food and water here. It looks as though it rained recently and we'll be able to find fresh water in those rock crevices. There should be plenty of fish too.' He began to search the rock pools.

Trang got back into the boat and spoke gently to his sister.

'Mimi. Wake up.'

At first there was no response and a cold fear gripped him. Surely just when the journey was over she wasn't going to slip away from him?

'Mimi! We've found land. We're safe.' He spoke urgently now, trying to sound confident.

Her lids flickered and she opened her eyes.

Banh came over and together they helped the feeble, emaciated girl out of the boat and carried her to a grassy patch where they laid her gently under a tree.

'There now,' said Trang. 'You can rest here and presently we'll find something for you to eat. Just think what it will be like to have a really good meal at last. Banh and I will catch some fish.'

Mimi smiled. 'I'm not hungry, Trang, but fish for yourselves.'

Banh was already lying on the rocks, peering down into the water and he went over to join him.

'Crabs, jelly fish and squid,' said Banh.

'We'll give the jelly fish a miss,' grinned Trang. 'Let's see what else we can catch.'

As they kept quite still some small fish swam into sight just below them. Banh dangled his hand in the water and watched them then, like lightning, he tossed a fish in the air so that it landed struggling on the rocks. Banh grabbed it and struck it on the head. Soon between them they had enough for a meal. They were ravenous and tearing the raw flesh in their fingers they feasted as they had not done for weeks. Only by eating occasional strands of floating seaweed had they survived.

Taking a small piece of flesh between his fingers, Trang offered it to his sister. 'Eat, Mimi. You must eat and you'll grow stronger.'

She had no appetite but to please him she tried, though he could see it sickened her.

It was almost dark when they went down to the shore but a moon was rising, covering the island in a brilliant light. The tide had come in and the boat was floating, bumping against the rocks. They pulled it in and shortened the rope before taking out their few possessions. Then, exhausted after their exertions, they stretched out beside the girl and fell asleep.

* * * * *

The sound of the sea washing the shore woke

Trang. It was a few moments before he realised where he was. Dawn was creeping up from the East, the grey light outlining the rocky coast and the trees on the hill behind him. The island was colourless, stark and barren. Only the cry of the gulls and the sound of the breaking waves disturbed the silence.

The other two were still sleeping. Trang got up and walked down to the water. He felt its pleasant sensation washing over his feet, and the sand dragging at his toes as the water receded. Out to sea there was nothing, only the horizon and the two islands he had noticed the evening before. Perhaps some fishermen lived on them. There must be someone who could tell them where they were. Until then it would be unwise to put to sea again.

He listened. In the distance he could hear a motor. As he watched, a trawler came into sight round the cove. On board were three fishermen. One was at the wheel, the other two worked at the nets. Trang shouted and waved. Immediately they saw him and changed direction, switching off the engine. As they came close one shouted across the water in Chinese.

'What are you doing here? Are you alone?'

'We need help,' shouted Trang. The men consulted briefly and then one of them got into a dinghy and rowed towards him.

'How long have you been here?' the fellow asked, stroking the water with his oars.

Trang was cautious. 'We landed last night. Our boat is leaking and my sister is ill.' He pointed to where Mimi lay under the trees. Banh was awake now and came down to join him.

The fisherman looked at them closely. 'Where are you from?' he asked.

'Vietnam.'

'One of the boat people then? You came all the way in that?'

'There were more of us and we set off in a trawler,' Trang explained. 'We were swept off course by a storm four days after we left. One night we were boarded by pirates and they took everything we had and killed some of the men who tried to fight them off. They took some of our women too. The rest of us they cast off in two small boats but we lost sight of the others.'

'We've heard such things happen,' said the boat-man. 'It's a wonder you survived.'

'Our mother was with us. She died on the way,' said Trang.

'So now you're on your own. Where do you want to go?'

'Hong Kong Island. I must get help for my sister.'

'How is it you speak Chinese?' asked the man.

'My father's Chinese. There are a lot of us in Vietnam.'

'Have you friends or relatives here?'

'Be careful what you say,' warned Banh in Viet-namese. 'They might hand us over to the police.'

Trang felt that the man would be more likely to help if he spoke the truth.

'We know no one in Hong Kong,' he said.

The fisherman came closer. He was a man of about

fifty, small and wiry with a lined weather beaten face and sunken eyes.

'Look here,' he said. 'I'll be honest with you. We'd like to help but I have to warn you, you'll not be welcome in Hong Kong. Didn't you know that they're detaining all the boat people? They've been coming over in their thousands and we can't cope with so many. Now they put them in camps and send them back to where they came from.'

'I heard that but there was nowhere else to go. My father said that if we're political refugees we would be allowed to stay.'

'There are too many already. They all say they're political refugees escaping from the communist regime but in truth most of them are coming over because they think they can make money here.'

'We're willing to work,' said Trang.

'If you can find a job,' said the fisherman. 'Our own people are finding it hard enough to get work and in any case we'll soon have the Communists here. You might as well have stayed in your own country.'

'Please help us,' Trang begged. 'My sister is dying. Just point us in the direction of Hong Kong and we won't bother you. Tell us where we stand the best chance of landing unnoticed and how I can go about finding a doctor. All we want is food and shelter till we find work.'

'Have you money?'

Trang shook his head. 'What we had was taken,' he said. Then a thought occurred to him. 'My father is a fisherman,' he said, 'and I've fished all my life. Would you have work for me?'

'You don't know what you're asking,' said the fisherman but his eyes were sympathetic, 'but I'll speak to my mates.'

Trang watched, anxious now lest the men might decide to report their arrival. They seemed to be arguing about the matter. He turned and went back to Mimi She was awake and was looking up at the tree.

'It's so good to see trees again after such a long time,' she whispered. She looked so ill, her skin stretched over high cheek bones. Her usually bright eyes were dull and her breathing shallow and rapid. He could tell from her high colour that she had a fever. He must get her to a doctor soon. Gently he persuaded her to sit up.

Two of the fishermen had returned to the shore and were talking to Banh. They had brought some food and water with them and offered it to Mimi, but she shook her head. She couldn't face anything solid but she sipped the water gratefully.

'We'll take you with us to Lamma Island and then decide what to do with you,' one of them said. 'You'll be safe there for a while. Let's get your sister on board first.' Trang helped as they carried her to the boat and rowed her out to the trawler.

'Do you trust them?' asked Banh as they waited. 'They'll probably get a reward for turning us in.'

'What alternative do we have?' asked Trang. 'We can't stay here.'

When the men returned, Trang asked if he could take the boat with him.

'Does it have an engine?'

'No,' he said. 'We came by sail, but there's not much left of them.'

'We'll leave the boat here. If it's leaking it's not going to be much good to us and it will only attract attention. We must keep out of the way of the Marine Police. If they see you, they might ask some awkward questions.'

When they were all on board, the fishermen pulled up anchor and started up the engine. Trang glanced once more towards the boat. He didn't want to leave it. It had brought them to safety and without it, they would lose their independence. Besides it was their last link with the past.

He glanced at Mimi. She looked better now and smiled sadly at him. He knew she was thinking of their mother. He went and sat beside her.

'As soon as you're better, Banh and I will find work and look for somewhere to live,' he said. 'I'm sure we'll manage all right.'

'I hope so,' she said. 'I just wish we could let Father know we're here. He'd be so proud of you.' Her face clouded. 'Oh Trang, I wonder if we'll ever be together again?'

'Of course we will,' said Trang. 'Father promised that he and Ky would follow as soon as they could, didn't he?'

But he said it to comfort Mimi. He had little faith that with the perils of the journey they would ever see their father and elder brother again.

Chapter 2

As the days passed Trang felt his strength returning and he began to put on weight. Ah Soon the fisherman, had lost no time in putting them to work, taking Trang on fishing expeditions while Banh was left to do other jobs about the place like mending nets and sorting out fishing tackle.

They had been given the use of a wooden shack where they could sleep and keep their things, but the tin roof leaked and the place was draughty. Lobster pots were piled along one side together with tins of paint and varnish and Ah Soon was in and out whenever he needed something.

It was quite unsuitable for Mimi. When he and Banh were working, she was left for hours on her own and though she never complained and spent a good deal of time sleeping, Trang knew it couldn't go on like this and something must be done.

'We'll have to find somewhere else for you,' Trang told her. 'You're never going to get better in this place.'

'I'm alright. I feel better already,' she insisted. 'That awful journey's over and now we have food and shelter of a sort and you've found work. What more could we wish for, Trang? Now we must write to father and tell

16

him about it. Once he arrives, we'll be able to find somewhere better to live.'

He was silent. It was better that she should have this hope to cling to.

'We must tell him about mother, too. You will write, won't you Trang?' She had a spasm of coughing which left her exhausted.

'You see what I mean,' he said. 'I don't think that old village doctor knows what's wrong with you. The medicine he gave you is useless. Mimi, I think you ought to be in hospital.'

'I don't expect there is one on this island.'

'There would be in Hong Kong. I could take you there.'

Mimi looked at him, alarmed. 'I don't want to go away from you,' she said. 'Please don't make me. I'll be better soon.' She gave him a thin smile.

'I won't promise,' he said firmly. One of them had to be strong. 'I shall speak to Ah Soon about it. 'We've got to get you fit and then we can make plans.'

He spoke to Banh first.

'I'm worried about Mimi,' he said. 'She should be in hospital.'

Banh brushed it aside. 'She's better already. Ah Soon got the doctor to her and he's satisfied, isn't he? Don't fuss, Trang. At least we have somewhere to stay now. Even a job though it's not exactly what I had in mind.'

Trang nodded. 'Perhaps not,' he said. 'But it's not bad for a start. In fact if it weren't for Mimi being ill, we could settle happily here. There's little likelihood of the police discovering us and I think Ah Soon finds us useful so he won't give us away.'

'Just the same,' said Banh. 'I don't intend to be a fisherman's assistant all my life. As soon as I get a chance I'm off to Hong Kong to see if I can't find work there.'

'We'll keep together though?' asked Trang, surprised that Banh should contemplate going off on his own.

'It's alright for you,' said Banh. 'You're a fisherman and Ah Soon finds you useful. I'm not. There's money to be made in Hong Kong. My father said so and one day I intend to make a good living there.'

Trang was silent. What Banh did was his own business. At the moment he was much more concerned about Mimi.

He let the idea rest for a few days and then it rained. Water came through the tin roof and trickled down the walls. Rivulets ran down the hill into the shack soaking the bedding and there was no dry place where Mimi could comfortably lie. Her cough worsened, racking her body and keeping Trang awake all through the night with anxiety.

He went to see Ah Soon. He found him in the kitchen, smoking a cigarette. He seemed preoccupied and somewhat annoyed at the interruption.

'I see little improvement in my sister,' Trang began.

'You can't expect quick results. You've got to give the treatment time to work.'

'She still has a high fever and she coughs all the time. The hut is very damp and I'm afraid she'll only get worse if we leave her where she is.'

'It's the best I can do for you. At least you have food and shelter. You should be grateful for that.'

'We are very grateful but I think my sister should go to hospital.'

Ah Soon took a long pull at his cigarette and exhaled slowly. 'You may be right,' he said presently. 'I wouldn't want to be responsible for her if she gets worse.'

'Then you'll help me to find somewhere for her?'

Ah Soon shook his head in a thoughtful manner. Then he cleared his throat and spat through the open door. 'It's not easy. She'll have to go to Hong Kong and that will cost money.'

'But I have none.'

'There are many sick people in Hong Kong. It's difficult to find a place and it won't be free.'

'Then what shall I do?' Ah Soon was becoming impatient with the problem but Trang wasn't giving up. 'Could the doctor find a place for her?' he pressed.

Ah Soon studied Trang thoughtfully, his sharp eyes sizing him up. 'I could perhaps help you but I'm not a rich man and I would expect some commitment from you.'

'What sort of commitment?'

'I'll be honest with you. You're useful to me on the boat and I think I can trust you. I'm asking you to work for me without payment for a while.'

'I'll do that,' said Trang. 'If I can take Mimi to

hospital and visit her sometimes, I'll do whatever I can to help you.'

'That would be unwise if you value your freedom. You'd do better to keep clear of Hong Kong. Once the authorities discover you're one of the boat people, they'll detain you.'

'But who will take her to hospital? She can't go alone.'

'I'll find someone to make the necessary arrangements for her.'

'No,' said Trang. 'She won't go without me. Besides I must see for myself that she's alright.'

'Very well then. It's up to you. If you want to go with her, you can but I want you back the next day. There's work to be done.'

He wanted to stay until he was quite sure that Mimi was comfortably settled but he daren't argue with Ah Soon.

'How do I get her there?' he asked.

'You'll have to take the ferry from the harbour and then find a taxi. I'll get the doctor to give you a note to the hospital.'

Trang thanked him for his trouble and went off to tell Mimi. The rain had stopped and the sun shone down from a blue sky. She was sitting outside the shack and was looking brighter. She was eating a little these days. They had a charcoal fire outside the shack and when he came back from work, he prepared small delicacies for her which she seemed to enjoy. She smiled at him as he sat down beside her.

'Ah Soon's making arrangements for you to go into hospital,' he told her.

Mimi's dark eyes expressed dismay. 'I'm getting better, Trang,' she protested. 'It's bound to take time. The doctor said so and I won't go anywhere without you.'

'I'm coming with you. I'll see that you're alright and then I'll have to come back here to help Ah Soon. We owe him for his hospitality and for looking after us.'

Banh was just coming up from the boat and sat down on an old cane chair they had scrounged from a rubbish dump.

'I'm taking Mimi to hospital tomorrow,' Trang told him.

'I'll stay here then till you get back but I want to go myself and look for a job. In fact we might both find employment over there,' he added. 'It would be much more convenient than this out of the way place.'

Trang shook his head. 'I promised I'd work for Ah Soon for nothing as he's fixing up the hospital,' he explained.

Banh frowned. 'How long will you have to do that?' he asked.

Trang shrugged. 'I don't know. A month perhaps,' he suggested. 'Listen Banh. I'm prepared to go along with this for the time being but if you want to go off on your own, there's nothing to stop you.'

'I don't want to be a nuisance,' Mimi interrupted. 'I can't help it at the moment and I know you're right about the hospital. I must go along with this but as soon as I'm better I'll find a job.'

'You're only fifteen, nothing more than a school girl,' said Trang, teasing her fondly. 'What sort of work could you do?'

'I don't know till I try, do I? There're quite a few things I can think of.'

* * * * *

The next day they took Mimi to the ferry. She could walk short distances very slowly but by the time they had found her a seat on the boat she was exhausted and coughing again.

Ah Soon came with them. He had a word with the boatman and paid their fares. Then he gave Trang a few dollars. 'You'll need this for food and your return fare,' he said. 'I'll expect you back tomorrow.'

It was a short crossing and as they reached the harbour they were amazed by the variety of craft hurrying over the water between Hong Kong and Kowloon. Ferries and fishing junks with vast brown sails, small boats paddled by coolies, and looking across the water to Kowloon they could see great ocean liners berthed there. Trang gazed in amazement at the tightly packed high rise buildings which dominated the Hong Kong waterfront. Behind them rose a green mountain with groups of grand looking houses dotted about the slopes.

'What a thrilling place,' said Mimi, excitement in her voice. 'When I'm fit, we'll have a great time exploring it.' Then her face clouded. 'I wish Mother could have seen it. We could have had such fun together.'

'Perhaps one day we can show Father and Ky

around.' Trang said it without conviction but the thought cheered Mimi.

The ferry tied up at the quayside and Trang helped his sister slowly up the steps. It was going to be a long time, he thought, before she was well enough to do anything other than rest. He told her to sit down and wait while he went off and found a taxi.

'Wanchai,' he told the driver. 'We want the hospital.'

He showed the man the address which was sprawled in Chinese characters across the envelope which Ah Soon had given him. He had no idea how much this trip would cost but there was no alternative. Mimi couldn't walk that far.

Progress was slow. The roads were congested with slow moving traffic which filled the air with exhaust fumes. Trams rattled along the metal tracks and bicycles wove their way amongst pedestrians who spilled into the road in danger of oncoming cars. This must be the most crowded city in the world, thought Trang.

They passed rows of shops and open fronted stores until they came to an industrial area. Here Trang saw signs indicating that they had reached Wanchai and the driver turned down a narrow street and stopped in front of a tall grey building.

'Hospital,' he said.

Trang paid the fare which left him with little enough to buy a meal. He had never been into a hospital before but over the last few weeks he had become familiar with illness as first his mother and then Mimi sickened and grew weaker. He shuddered as it all came back to him and he was filled with a desperate sense of loneliness. If he lost Mimi he couldn't bear it. She was all he had now.

He led her into the dark interior of the hospital and handed in the note at Reception. It was a gloomy place and he hated the thought of leaving her here for days by herself. He followed as they wheeled her along corridors until they reached a women's ward. The place seemed terribly overcrowded and patients, some of them looking seriously ill, lay along the corridors waiting for a bed.

Finding a vacant space, he told Mimi to sit down while he went off for a nurse.

'Your sister?' she asked, writing down details.

'Yes.'

'Address?'

He thought for a moment and then gave his name followed by Ah Soon's. 'That will find me,' he said. 'He's a fisherman on Lamma Island.'

'Lamma Island,' she said. 'She could have been treated there. They have a clinic.'

'I know but she needs nursing. I was advised to send her here. We haven't been in Hong Kong long.'

Mimi looked at him and he caught her meaning. Don't say too much.

'I'll come back tomorrow and see how she is,' he told the nurse.

'There's no need,' said Mimi. 'I'm sure they'll get in touch with you if necessary. Ah Soon needs you and when the time comes I know I can find my own way back.'

'Nonsense. You won't be fit to travel on your own for a long time. I shall come and get you. Perhaps not for a while but be patient and have a good rest. You'll soon be strong again.'

The nurse left them and busied herself with her other patients.

'I'll drop in tomorrow and see you before I go back,' said Trang.

'Good,' whispered Mimi. In spite of her brave words, now it came to parting he knew how scared she was to be left alone and he could hardly bear it himself.

Outside he stood on the kerb of the main street, feeling isolated in a hostile world. The traffic, the bustle of this great metropolis confused him. He had been to cities in his own country but they were nothing like this. Here there was an urgency about people as though they had little time to finish their business.

Someone touched his arm. 'You look lost.'

By now Trang knew that there was danger in admitting to being a newcomer. He tried to look at ease in these unfamiliar surroundings.

'No. I was waiting for someone,' he said.

'People who know the place, don't stare up at the Peak, or look about them with amazement written all over their faces. They've seen it all before,' the young man said. He had a pleasant face and spoke with a smile. 'If you want help, I might be able to offer it. Otherwise just tell me to shove off. I'll take the hint.'

Trang decided to risk it. 'I'm looking for some-where to sleep, just for the night,' he said.

'Come with me. I think I know somewhere.'

Trang fell into step beside him.

'I haven't much money,' he said. 'It will have to be somewhere cheap.'

'Don't worry. There are places to suit everybody's price range. What's your name? Mine's Cheng.'

'Trang. I'm a fisherman on Lamma Island.'

'That explains it,' said Ah Cheng. 'I wondered about your accent. If you didn't speak Chinese so well, I would put you down as one of the boat people. There are a lot of Vietnamese about these days though they don't often slip through the net.'

He looked at Trang who firmly shook his head.

'You're wrong,' he said, perhaps a shade too quickly.

Ah Cheng shrugged. 'Don't worry,' he said. 'I'm not a policeman.'

They passed some cheap restaurants and beer houses and then a pawn shop. Trang glanced at his watch. If he was desperate he could always sell it.

At last Ah Cheng turned into a tall building. The ground floor was full of Indian shops offering cheap clothing and trinkets. He ignored these and made for the stairs, taking them two at a time and Trang, still weak after his ordeal at sea, had difficulty in keeping up. As they went up floor after floor they passed offices and health parlours and small businesses behind closed doors. At last Ah Cheng paused to wait for him.

'Up here you'll find rooms for as little as twenty dollars,' he said. 'You'll just have to keep trying till you

26

find a vacancy.'

'But I haven't got that much,' said Trang.

'You won't find anything cheaper.'

'Then I'll have to make do without a bed,' said Trang. He had noticed a number of down and outs, sleeping in various parts of the building. They were part of the scene and people ignored them. He could join them.

'Like that, is it?' asked Ah Cheng. 'Well, I suppose you can take your luck with the rest of them if it's only for a night. I'll have to leave you here as I have work to do.'

'What are the chances of getting a job here?' asked Trang.

'Not good. A word of warning though. No matter what you say, it stands out a mile that you're a newcomer and there are gangs on the look out for people like you. They're dangerous. Once they get you into their clutches, you'll find it hard to escape. Just take care from whom you accept favours.' And with that, Ah Cheng ran down the stairs and disappeared in the crowd before Trang had time to thank him.

It was getting dark and he was famished. He went back to the street and bought a bowl of noddles which he devoured. Then, finding a vacant place on one of the floors, he pulled his jacket round him and curled up on the concrete. The hardness was familiar. His body had become resilient to discomfort and accustomed to extremes of heat and cold. He was able to snatch what sleep he needed at a moment's notice and he had no problem now.

He awoke early the next morning and searched the back streets for a standpipe. He found one on a piece of derelict land and joined the queue. When his turn came he had a drink and dashed water over his neck and face. Then he set off for the hospital.

He saw Mimi straight away and her face brightened at the sight of him.

'Trang. Where did you sleep? I've been so worried about you.'

'No need. I was quite comfortable and I've had something to eat. What about you?'

'Already I feel better. You mustn't worry about me. I'm going to be all right. You go to Ah Soon. He's been good to us and you should help him out.'

'In a couple of weeks I'll get some time off and come and see how you're getting on. Perhaps by then you'll be well enough to come back with me and we can make plans. We'll have to find somewhere else to live. You can't stay in that shack.'

'We could do it up perhaps. Make it more habitable. Trang, you won't forget to write to father, will you?'

'I've been thinking about that and wondering if it would be wise? If I write home with a Hong Kong stamp it might be intercepted and he'd be in trouble. You know how worried he was because he thought he was being watched. He always expected the worse.'

Mimi shook her head. 'No matter how dangerous it is, we should try and let him know we're here and besides we must tell him about Mother.'

'He might give up hope if he knows about that but

I think you're right. I will send a letter.'

She lay back, relieved.

'Mimi, I must go now.' He took her hands, searching her face. She certainly did look a little better. Next time he came she would be looking more like the beautiful girl he remembered, though he suspected she might never lose that sad expression after all she had been through.

'Hurry up and get well, Mimí,' he whispered and then to his dismay he felt tears coming. He turned quickly before she could see and walked down the ward. He paused at the entrance to give her a brief wave and she lifted her hand.

Chapter 3

Trang found Ah Soon preparing the boat for a fishing expedition.

'How did it go?' the fisherman asked, looking up briefly from his task.

'All right,' said Trang. 'My sister seems happy enough. I gave them your address so they'll let us know when she's ready to leave. They couldn't tell me how long it would be but I promised to go over and see her.'

'It takes time and money to go to Hong Kong. She knows how to get here and she'll turn up when she's ready.'

'But I must go and visit her,' said Trang. 'She doesn't know anyone over there and she's bound to be lonely. Even when she's better I would never let her come back here on her own. She wouldn't find her way.'

Ah Soon was unsympathetic. 'Of course she would. She can ask, can't she?'

Trang said nothing. He wasn't going to argue but he didn't intend to wait till then. He would give it two weeks and then ask if he could go over and see her.

'You'd better get some sleep,' said the fisherman. 'We'll be leaving on a fishing trip this evening and we won't be back for three days. Go to the cottage and ask my wife to give you enough food and drinks for four people. Bring it down here and load it into the boat.'

Trang did as he was told and piled the containers neatly where they would keep dry. Then he went off to find Banh. He was sitting outside the shack eating fruit.

'How did you find Hong Kong?' he asked.

'I'm famished,' said Trang, reaching for a banana. 'I didn't like it. It was crowded, noisy and very nerve-wracking.' He gave Banh an account of his trip.

'What about jobs?'

Trang shook his head. 'I was talking to a fellow who seemed to know his way around and he told me it wasn't easy to find work. He said there were criminal gangs about and that you had to be careful who you got involved with. It might be better to stay here for a while, Banh, until we see how things go.'

'I'm bored already with this place. I want to go and see for myself. Ah Soon doesn't really need me here and he might give me some advice. He seems to have connections.'

Trang said nothing. He had to stay for the time being. Then, once Mimi was better and he had worked off his debt, he could think again.

Four of them went down to the trawler that evening, leaving Banh to do some repairs on one of the boats. Ah Soon's brother, a swarthy fellow with a limp, took charge of the boat. 'He was involved in a fight and got the worst of it,' explained Ah Soon, glancing in his direction but the fellow didn't seem inclined to enlarge on the story. He was an uncommunicative sort of man and Trang felt he would do well to steer clear of him. Ah Soon

31

nodded towards the other fisherman, a lad little older than himself. 'That's his son,' he said.

They motored through the night heading east. 'Where are we going?' asked Trang.

'We're meeting up with another fishing trawler,' Ah Soon said. 'They want us to take some goods to Hong Kong. After that we shall put out the nets. There are some good hauls to be had in that area. The Hong Kong waters are over fished and soon there'll be nothing left.'

'Aren't there laws about fishing rights?' asked Trang.

Ah Soon spat, directing his aim well over the side of the boat. 'If we all stuck to the rules, none of us would make a living,' he said. 'We have to make the little extra where we can. Everybody does it. You'll learn that in time.'

Round about dusk they came to an isolated island with deep rocky coves and Ah Soon turned towards it. To Trang's surprise there was a boat already moored there. They were obviously expected. They dropped anchor some way off shore and Ah Soon lowered the dinghy and told them to wait for him. He stayed some time talking to the men and then they started to load some packages into the dinghy. After a while Ah Soon rowed back.

'Put these packages in strong plastic bags,' he told Trang, 'and store them deep in the bows where they won't get wet.'

'What is it?' asked Trang.

'Some sort of cooking agent,' said Ah Soon. 'Comes from the mainland and it's highly valued in

Chinese cooking.'

Trang thought it was a long way to come to pick up some ingredient that could be shipped on an ordinary cargo boat to Hong Kong but he had already learnt that Ah Soon was not a man who liked to be questioned too closely. He would ask one of the other fishermen some-time.

When they were well clear of the island, Ah Soon ordered the nets to be thrown overboard and for the next few hours they trawled, bringing in heavy catches. Every man was required to haul the fish onto the boat where it was put into containers with enormous blocks of ice to keep them fresh.

'A good haul,' said Ah Soon with satisfaction. 'Now let's make for Hong Kong.'

They were well on their way when one of the fisherman shouted, 'A patrol boat coming up on your starboard!'

Ah Soon wasted no time. He barked out an order. 'Give her full throttle.'

Trang was amazed at the turn of speed. The marine police patrol boat had been coming towards them at a good speed but already the trawler was outstripping it. Trang had examined the powerful engine a few days ago when he was doing some maintenance on the boat, and thought that such an expensive piece of machinery was quite unnecessary for a fishing trawler. When he had questioned Ah Soon about it he was told that speed meant valuable time could be saved. Now, though, Trang saw another use for it. The trawler had left the patrol boat way behind.

He breathed a sigh of relief. Had the launch caught up with them, the police might have asked him some awkward questions. He must always be on his guard against that.

The close encounter seemed to have left Ah Soon nervous and he kept looking back. As they neared Hong Kong, he directed his brother to motor between some islands to give the patrol boat time to get on its way. The area seemed familiar to Trang and then he recognised the island on which they had landed. But although he searched the cove for his boat it was too well hidden for him to see.

'Some time we'll come back for it but not today,' said Ah Soon, following Trang's gaze. 'She'll be safe enough there.'

There was a lot of activity on the water this early morning. Other fishing vessels were making harbour and some big yachts owned by wealthy foreigners were heading out to sea from the Royal Hong Kong Yacht Club.

When they reached the fish market quay Ah Soon brought the trawler alongside and tied up. Coolies waited to transfer the container onto trolleys and wheel them into the market. Trang wondered whether he dare ask Ah Soon if he could slip away for a while to see Mimi, but then he thought better of it. He couldn't expect them to wait for him and besides he was needed here just now.

He stayed on board till they reached the fishing village on Lamma Island where they unloaded the nets. Trang noticed that the packages were still hidden in the bows. He began to bring them out.

'Leave them,' said Ah Soon. 'We're delivering them later on. You can go ashore here, Trang, to sort out the nets.'

'The other three men remained on board and Trang was surprised to see the trawler continue past the harbour and along the coast. Trang watched it for a while and then went off in search of Banh.

'Is Ah Soon running some other business besides fishing?' he asked casually.

'Why do you ask?'

'On this trip we met up with a fishing boat on an island miles away and they took some packages on board. Ah Soon said it was some kind of cooking ingredient but on the way back he was very worried about a police launch coming in our direction. I just wondered if he was dealing in something other than fish.'

'You mean he might be smuggling?'

Trang shrugged. 'Don't know. A lot of that sort of thing goes on here specially if there's money to be made. Have you noticed that engine? It's incredibly powerful. Far more than is needed on a fishing boat. It must have cost a fortune and if he's as poor as he says he is, I don't know how he can afford it.'

'Why not ask him about it? There must be an explanation.'

'If it's something illegal he wouldn't be likely to tell us, would he? I don't think we should let him know we suspect anything.'

'Not unless he needs our help,' said Banh. 'Then there might be something in it for us.'

35

Trang frowned. 'If that's the case, I don't think we should have anything to do with it. If he was caught we'd be in trouble as well. We've got enough problems as it is.'

For the next two weeks he put the matter from his mind. Ah Soon kept him fully occupied. They went out on fishing trips most nights and then there was all the maintenance on the nets and boats. Lobster pots had to be put out and regularly checked, then the contents put in containers and sent to the big hotels in Hong Kong. It was familiar work to Trang and he was good at it. It wasn't long before Ah Soon was giving him more responsibility whenever he was away. He had been over to Hong Kong twice lately leaving Trang in charge of the boats.

As he had promised Mimi, he eventually wrote to his father. It was some time before he could bring himself to write about the terror and sadness of those days at sea. At the top of the letter, he wrote Ah Soon's name and village.

'Dear Father,' he began, 'You will be glad to know that we have arrived on Lamma Island after many days at sea. It was a terrible journey and the sad thing that I must tell you is that Mother died. As you know she wasn't well when we left and I think the anxiety of leaving you and worrying about the future was too much for her. We put her gently overboard. It was all we could do.'

Unfortunately we lost the boat. We were boarded by pirates not long after we left and they took everything. Some of the men were wounded in the fight and the pirates took others away with them. There was nothing we could do. In the end they put the rest of us in a couple of small dinghies with a little food and water and let us go. We had a sick child with us who died shortly afterwards and then Mother. Mimi took it very hard and by the time we reached an island and were rescued by some fishermen, she was very ill. I took her to hospital and I hope she'll soon be better.

The hope of seeing you and Ky again one day keeps her going. I promise I will care for her as you and Mother would want me to. I have a job as a fisherman and we live in a shack near the harbour.'

He sat thoughtfully for a while and then decided that he had given all the information necessary. He ended, 'We speak of you often and send all our love, Trang.'

He sealed the letter and posted it at the village post office. He'd had to borrow small amounts of money from Banh for the stamp and other shopping because at the moment, he was the only one earning. At the same time he enquired if there was a letter from the hospital. He was sure that Mimi would let him know when she was allowed to leave.

At the end of three weeks he could bear the wait no longer and asked Ah Soon if he could go and see her.

'You'll hear when she's to be discharged.' Ah Soon was irritable these days as though he had something on his mind. 'Just at the moment I can't spare you. My brother's away and I need you here.'

He was considering what to do when Banh told him that he had been given some time off.

'What are you going to do?' asked Trang.

'Going over to Hong Kong. I want to go and see about a job.'

'Then could you go and see Mimi?' asked Trang eagerly.

'I will if I have time. I've only got a few hours.'

'Please try, Banh,' he urged. ' I promised to go and see her but Ah Soon won't give me time off. She'll be wondering what's happened to us.'

'I'll try and fit it in but I can't promise.'

Trang didn't remind him that there was a time when he couldn't see enough of Mimi. He wasn't the only one. Lots of his friends thought Mimi lovely but she wasn't particularly interested in any one of them. She had plenty of friends but she was happiest when she was with her family and of course, her cat. In spite of all they had been through together, it seemed that now Mimi was sick, Banh had no further interest in her.

He said no more about it until he saw Banh that evening.

'How did you find Hong Kong?' he asked.

'Like you said, overcrowded. Not much chance of a job there. I walked for miles but as soon as I asked for work, they asked to see my identity card. Where do you get one of those?'

'I don't know,' said Trang. 'Did you see Mimi?'

Banh shook his head, looking somewhat embarrassed.

'There just wasn't time. I was on the other side of town and it would have taken too long to reach the hospital. I'm sorry, Trang. Next time perhaps.'

Trang said no more. He felt that Banh had let him down. He made up his mind that he wasn't going to wait any longer.

'I must go,' he told Ah Soon. 'My sister will wonder what's happened.'

'You can go in a couple of days. Ah Lo will be back by then. You've worked well, Trang, and you deserve a day off.'

* * * * *

He took the ferry to Hong Kong and then walked to the hospital. Ah Soon had given him some money but he needed that for a taxi if he was to bring Mimi back with him.

He went straight to the ward but he could not immediately see her. She must have been moved. He went to ask a nurse, an older woman with an expressionless face.

'I'm looking for my sister, Mimi Van Bon?' he said. 'Where is she?'

'She left a few days ago,' the nurse said.

'But why wasn't I told? She wasn't well enough to get home on her own.'

'There was nothing we could do about it,' said the nurse. 'She discharged herself.'

'But I'm sure she would have let me know if she was leaving. I told her I would fetch her. Did she say that she was coming home?'

'I told you, she discharged herself. Patients who do that are no longer our responsibility.'

'But she must have left a message. An address or

something?' Trang was shouting. He was desperate.

'Just mind who you're speaking to, young man,' she said. 'I'm only a nurse here. It has nothing to do with me.'

'I'm sorry. But she's my sister. How am I going to find her?'

'She'll be on her way home, I expect.'

'But that was days ago and we haven't seen her yet. How well was she?'

'Better, but not well enough to be discharged. Don't worry though. She was fit enough to make the journey.'

'Perhaps she spoke to someone else about it. Please could you find out?'

'I'll ask the sister.' The woman went off and Trang saw her in the office talking to another nurse. They took a while discussing it and sometimes they looked in his direction. He thought they must be deciding what to tell him. Presently the nurse returned with Mimi's jacket.

'There's no message, but she left this,' she said, handing it to him.

'So you can do nothing to help?' said Trang, glaring at her. 'All right but if I can't find her I shall come back. I shall insist on seeing the doctor. I don't believe you should allow a young girl out by herself when she's ill.'

He left the ward and went slowly down the stairs and out onto the street. A gulf of hot air came up to meet him. He felt terribly responsible. Mimi had grown tired of waiting and had decided to find her own way back. But what had happened to her on the way?

Chapter 4

Ah Soon was unconcerned when Trang told him about Mimi's disappearance.

'She'll turn up,' he said. 'Perhaps she's got herself a job.'

'How could she?' Trang demanded. 'She's ill. The nurse said she should never have left the hospital.'

'Then why did she leave? Did you ask them?'

'Of course I did,' said Trang, exasperated. 'I can tell you why she left. Because she thought she was forgotten. I said I'd come back in a couple of weeks and you refused to let me go. It was over a month since I'd seen her.'

'You're being unreasonable. I've given you work and made arrangements for your sister to go into hospital. Now you're blaming me because the girl discharged herself instead of waiting. It's her own fault.'

'I'm sorry,' said Trang. 'I am grateful for what you've done for us. It's just that I'm so worried about Mimi. She's disappeared in a strange place. She knows nobody and she's far from well. Of course I'm worried about her. Please help me to find her. You're the only one who can.'

Ah Soon was thoughtful. Then he cleared his throat and spat.

'You're right in thinking that a young girl on her own in Hong Kong is unsafe although you can't hold me responsible for that. She might have got herself a job. Have you thought of that? There's little we can do but wait. If we report this to the police they would question you and you don't want that.'

'But something must have happened to her. She's not well and the longer I leave it, the harder it will be to find her. I shall have to go and look for her.'

'You'd be wasting your time. Where would you begin your search in a place like Hong Kong?' asked Ah Soon. 'No. You'll have to wait. She knows where to find you. Now, try and put it out of your mind. There's work to be done. I want two cans of fuel taken down to the trawler.'

Trang carried it down and filled up the engine, thinking over what Ah Soon had said. There might be some truth in his suggestion that Mimi had got herself a job. She would want to start earning if she could and someone might have offered her work. But as he returned from his task, he knew he couldn't stay around here just hoping that she would turn up. She could be in all sorts of trouble and she wouldn't be able to help herself.

He found Banh nailing boards across a gap in the shed.

'It will keep out some of the weather,' he said.

'Mimi's disappeared,' Trang told him.

'What do you mean disappeared? She's in hospital, isn't she?'

'No. She's left. I've got to find her. Will you come with me?'

Banh shook his head. 'No. I can't. I've work to do here.'

'But that's nothing compared with finding Mimi. Don't you understand how serious it is, Banh? She's gone and no one seems to know where she is.'

Banh shrugged. 'She knows where to find you. She'll turn up when she's ready.'

'How can you be so calm about it? I thought you cared for Mimi?'

'Of course I do but we've got to be sensible about it. There must be a good reason why she left the hospital.'

'Banh, please help. We've got to stick together. No-one else is going to bother about us.'

'I'm sorry, Trang. I really am but one of us ought to work and bring in some money. I think I might even do better in future. Ah Soon has offered me a job in Hong Kong.'

'What sort of job?'

'Well it's not exactly in Hong Kong, but I would have to go there sometimes. He's got some sort of a business over there and he needs a messenger.'

Trang was puzzled. 'Tell me more,' he said.

'I can't say too much at present but Ah Soon thinks I'm the sort of fellow he can trust and if I'm any good at it I'd work on a commission basis. He'd pay me so much for each job I did. I'd make more that way but I'm not sure yet what I'd be doing exactly.'

'If you're going to Hong Kong, you'd be able to

help me look for Mimi.'

'If I get a chance,' said Banh. 'But I can't come with you now. Couldn't you wait for a bit?'

'No.' Trang had lost patience. He could no longer rely on Banh. He went off to find Ah Soon.

'I've got to find my sister,' he said. 'When I've found her I'll work for you again.'

'I need you now,' said the fisherman. 'If I can't depend on you on a regular basis, you're no use to me. If you're determined to go, you might find that when you come back, there's no longer a place for you here.'

'I'm sorry. There's nothing more I can do about it,' said Trang.

He borrowed a few dollars for his immediate needs from Banh and promised to pay it back as soon as he could. Then he took the ferry across to Hong Kong.

Where to begin his search? He needed a job and he thought he would stand a better chance than Banh. In spite of what he had said about identity cards, he felt sure that if he was determined he would find some sort of employment, perhaps on a temporary basis.

His first call must be to the hospital. He made his way there, passing the pawn shop. He stopped and went in. Taking off the watch his father had given him, he asked the old Chinese behind the counter how much it was worth.

'I'll give you sixty dollars,' said the man, inspecting it.

'I'll take it,' said Trang. It would last him for quite a while.

44

At the hospital, he made enquiries but nothing had been heard of Mimi. She left without permission, they reminded him, and it was no longer their responsibility.

'May I speak to her doctor?'

There are many doctors,' said the Ward Sister. 'It would be difficult to find out which ones saw her and none of them would be able to give you information. We've checked the records which state that she had discharged herself.'

Trang spent the next few days aimlessly walking the streets in the hope of catching a glimpse of her and at night he returned to his old sleeping place in the Arcade.

One day he was standing on the street pretending to look in a shop window, yet in reality keeping a close watch as people hurried past. He was suddenly aware of a short fellow with glasses and greying hair standing next to him.

'Didn't I see you about here yesterday?' the man asked.

Trang shook his head. 'No.'

'And the day before? You make a habit of standing around here. Are you looking for someone?'

Trang decided to risk it. 'I'm looking for my sister,' he said. 'She left hospital and I don't know where's she gone.'

'That can happen here,' said the man with some sympathy. 'Does she know her way about?'

'No,' said Trang. 'We haven't been in Hong Kong very long. We live on Lamma Island. I don't know where to start looking.'

'Have you tried the police?'

'No,' said Trang.

'On the other hand unless you want to answer a lot of questions, it's not much use. Is she really your sister or is it girl friend trouble?'

'I told you, she's my sister.'

'Well, it's no use standing around waiting,' the man said. 'Would you be interested in a job?'

Trang hesitated. He was willing to try anything. The money he'd got for the watch wasn't going to last for ever.

'I might be,' he said.

'What's your trade?'

'I'm a fisherman but I can do most things.'

'Interested in factory work? Making small parts for bicycles? You won't earn much but most people are glad to get any kind of work these days.'

No question of an identity card and a job was a job and one thing led to another. He decided to chance it.

It didn't take him long to learn about work on the production line but it was deadly boring. He wasn't going to complain though. He worked hard and sometimes did a bit of overtime. The foreman was a decent enough fellow and kept a kindly eye on him.

After he had been there for a while, he took Trang aside and asked him if he would like to work on the electric lathe.

'It will mean a rise in your wages. You're a good worker. If you keep this up you'll find us fair.'

Trang thanked him.

'Where are you living?' asked the foreman.

Trang didn't want to admit that he slept rough every night. At the moment he couldn't afford accommodation. 'I've found lodgings in Wanchai,' he said.

'If you've been talking to the other fellows here, you'll probably know that most of them belong to a society?'

Trang shook his head. 'What sort of society?'

'It's a way of showing your loyalty to the firm and there are certain benefits attached to it. You could call it a kind of insurance. Are you interested?'

Trang shook his head. He had no intention of making his future in this job. 'I'll think about it,' he said.

'You'd be well advised to do that,' said the foreman. 'Unless you do you may well find yourself in difficulties.'

Trang thought about this as he ate his evening meal of rice and fish soup which he bought at the street stall. He managed quite well on one good meal a day and some fruit at lunchtime. If he chose fruit that was over ripe the stall holder would often let him have it for nothing.

He had also bought himself a pair of jeans, a shirt and some sandals which though cheap took the greater part of his week's wages. His clothes were threadbare now and the feel of the new garments against his skin brought back memories of drawers full of shirts and pullovers. That thought led on to his mother's cooking and meals with the family. It was hard to believe that they were gone forever. Now he only had Mimi...

47

He brought himself up sharply. No good could come of this. Two weeks had gone by since he had come over here and he was no nearer to finding her.

The factory hours were long and at the end of a day he had little energy left but every evening he tramped the streets in search of her.

He tried to do it in a systematic manner, covering a different area each night but for all he knew she might have passed by on the other side of the street. He would never see her in these crowds. He had no clue as to which part this vast over-crowded metropolis might prove most profitable.

Every night he returned to his place in the Arcade, tired and dispirited. He had got to know a few of the regulars who slept there, most of them drug addicts or people like himself, who could afford nothing better. He found them poor company, wrapped up in their own problems with little interest in the outside world.

One evening after leaving work, he walked once again past the hospital, wondering whether to call in again in the hope of picking up some information, some clue which might set him on the right track. But he wandered past and turned down a narrow alleyway leading to the waterfront. He stood here for a while wondering if Mimi had come this way when she left the hospital. Then an awful thought occurred to him. Perhaps she had been picked up by the police and put into a detention camp. How would he ever know?

He stood looking out over the water. Further along the quayside small boats tied up amongst the great fishing junks tossed in the wash of passing boats. It was getting dark and boats criss-crossed the harbour, each with their own bright lights. Across the road from the quay were narrow open-fronted shops and dark entrances leading to crowded tenement rooms.

'New here?' a voice at his elbow asked him.

Trang swung round to face a thickset Chinese in his mid-twenties with small narrow eyes and a scar down the right side of his face. He had a companion with him, a tall lanky fellow with a moustache.

'No,' said Trang. 'Just waiting for someone.'

'Who would that be?' asked the thickset fellow.

'My sister,' said Trang. There was no point in being rude. These days he was ready to talk to anyone in case he might learn something useful.

'Like working for the Pa Loom bicycle factory, do you?' asked the fellow casually.

Startled by this, Trang took another look at him. He had never seen the man before. 'How do you know where I work?' he asked.

'My name's Lee Tong and I probably know more about you than you think. For example your name is Trang Van Bon.'

'Why should you be interested in me?' asked Trang with an uneasy feeling that he might be talking to a policeman.

'I would suggest that you are one of the Vietnamese boat people so you wouldn't want to be too friendly with the police, would you?'

'I don't see why not,' Trang feigned innocence.

'That doesn't answer my question. Where did you get your information?'

Lee Tong ignored this. 'Perhaps we could help you find your sister.'

'You know where she is?' asked Trang. He felt very uneasy with this man but if Lee Tong knew where Mimi was, then he was prepared to go along with whatever he suggested.'

'Just a moment. Not so fast. First of all we have to find her and that takes time. We would expect payment.'

'How much?' asked Trang.

Lee Tong named a price equivalent to a week's wages. Trang readily agreed. 'When do you want it?' he asked

'Say, in three days time?'

Trang agreed. 'Tell me how you know about her?'

'I can tell you nothing. We have to find her first. Now give me some details.'

'She's small with shoulder length hair. She's wearing a red skirt and blouse and speaks Chinese. She has just come out of the hospital here in Wanchai. She's been very ill.'

'That will do as a start,' said Lee Tong. 'Thursday then. Meet you here at the same time.' He turned to go.

'Just a minute,' said Trang. 'Will you give her a message?'

'I might.'

'Then tell her that I will come for her as soon as I know where she is.'

Le Tong smiled then but Trang, searching for reassurance, could find no kindness in his smile.

Chapter 5

Over the next few days Trang tried to work out why Lee Tong should take such an interest in him. He felt sure that he already knew where Mimi was and that was why he had taken the trouble to find him. He wondered if Mimi had given him the information, but then she didn't know where he was working. It must have been someone else, someone perhaps at work.

Whatever were Lee Tong's motives, he would have to go along with him. It was his only contact with Mimi and once he knew where she was, he could go and see her himself. It was perfectly simple yet he could not quell his deep apprehension which increased as the time came for the meeting.

Trang waited for a long time on the quayside. He felt in his pocket. The money was safely there, wrapped in a piece of newspaper. He glanced about him and drew back into the shadows. He felt vulnerable under the street light.

It was almost dark and there were few people about. A couple of sailors had just passed by and not far away a group of youths were talking together by the steps that led down to the water. Every now and then they glanced in his direction. He seemed to be causing them some amusement.

He shivered. He had been in the factory all day working in intense heat. The deafening clank of machinery still rang in his ears. Here, on the waterfront, a cool breeze revived him but did little to quell his apprehension. He put on his jacket and began to walk slowly towards the pier where the Star ferries ran across to Kowloon.

Somewhere over there was mainland China. He wasn't sure how far it was, but in another few years Communist China would be taking over Hong Kong and it could be just as bad as Vietnam. For a moment he thought of home, a place where there was no freedom and people lived in constant fear of repression. Some of their friends who had resisted investigation from the authorities had been arrested and sent away, and his father was in constant danger when he helped people to escape.

Was life here really any better? It might be for the British and the wealthy Chinese but for people like Mimi and himself and the boat people in detention camps, had it been worth the risks and dangers of the voyage? His father had been mistaken. There was nothing here for them. They were not wanted but it was too late now to do anything about it.

He was filled with a longing for his family. There might be problems at home but they could be faced when they were together. One day soon he must call in at the post office on Lamma Island to see if there was a letter from his father. Perhaps even now he and Ky were on their way here. The thought cheered him.

'So you came?'

He would recognise that mocking voice anywhere. He took a hold of himself and turned to face Lee Tong. As before, he had brought along his assistant.

'Have you found my sister?' he demanded.

'Just a minute. Things aren't that easy. It took me a long time to find her. Fortunately I know the right people. Have you brought the money?'

'When you tell me...' His hand went into his pocket.

'I don't think you understand,' said Lee Tong in a measured tone. 'I am the one with the information for which you agreed to pay.'

It was no good arguing. Trang drew out the money and handed it over to Lee Tong, who counted it before shoving it into his pocket.

'I've found your sister. She's working in a bar. It's a good job and she likes it.'

Working in a bar? His gentle Mimi. She had no experience for a job like that.

'Where is it? Where can I find her?'

'She sent you a message. She says that you are not to look for her.'

'She would never say that. Tell me where she is and I'll find out for myself.'

'She doesn't want to see you.'

'I don't believe it.'

'Nevertheless you'll have to accept it. I've done what you asked and reassured you that she's alright. If that's her wish there's nothing more we can do.'

'How did you find her?' demanded Trang. 'How

could you possibly know where she is unless you already knew. And how did you find me? You know a lot more than you're letting on.'

Lee Tong shrugged. He turned to his assistant. 'Come on,' he said. 'Let's go.'

'Wait!' said Trang. 'If you're not going to help me, I shall go to the police.'

Lee Tong turned slowly to face him. 'People are disappearing every day and no-one knows where. Do you think it's wise to go to the police? You've no business to be here anyway. They're on the look out for people like you and they have a place to put them.'

Trang was defeated. What they said was true. He daren't risk it. No useful purpose could be served by standing up to these thugs. They might not even know where Mimi was, and what if they were stringing him along to get money out of him.

'What proof have I that you even saw my sister?' he asked. 'Frankly I don't believe you.'

'Very well,' said Lee Tong. 'We did what we could to help you and we could do more but if that's your attitude, we won't waste our time.'

He must take a grip on himself otherwise he would achieve nothing. He must try and get more information out of them because once they left, he would never see them again and at the moment they were his only chance of seeing Mimi.

'What do you mean by more?' he asked, trying to steady his voice.

'We could perhaps arrange a meeting, but only

with your sister's consent of course.'

'Then please will you do that.'

'It rather depends on how important she is to you.'

'Very important, of course. She's not well and I want to take her back to Lamma Island so that I can look after her.'

'I meant, what is it worth to you?'

'You're not going to make me pay again surely?'

'One hundred Hong Kong dollars to cover expenses,' said Lee Tong.

'That's ridiculous. I haven't got it.'

'Then find it. We'll give you till next week. If you haven't got it by then, the deal's off.'

There was no alternative. It was his only contact with Mimi. If he refused he might lose her for ever.

'I'll do it,' he said. 'Somehow I'll raise the money.'

He had no idea how he was to raise that much in time. He must intensify his search for Mimi. He still had a few days and there was always the hope that he might unexpectedly chance upon her.

All day he worked at the factory and spent most of the night walking the streets searching the crowds for the familiar face. He cut down on his food. By now he was utterly exhausted. Rather than waste time and energy going back to the arcade where he used to sleep, he lay down wherever he found himself and set off early the next day to arrive at work on time.

One night he had gone back to the centre of Hong Kong. This was an area frequented by Europeans and tourists. He often saw them gazing into expensive shop windows where jewellery, china and fashions were sold at exorbitant prices. The cost of one article would more than cover the amount demanded by Lee Tong.

He turned off into a narrow dimly lit street full of night clubs and bars. Glancing inside he saw men lying on couches smoking pipes and he recognised the sweet cloying smell of opium. Men stood guard outside the dens to give warning in case of a police raid. Presently he came out onto a brightly lit street. Music blared from dance halls and blue neon lights advertised the entertainment inside. There was no traffic here but people strolled along in a leisurely manner.

Then suddenly, far ahead of him, he thought he saw Mimi. He called out to her and she looked round. For a moment he thought she recognised him but then she turned away and was lost in the crowd. By the time he had reached the spot, she had vanished. He spent the next few hours in a fruitless search and then, exhausted he pulled his jacket round him and sank down in a shop entrance. In despair, he brushed the dampness from his cheeks and found that he was crying.

* * * * *

The following night he was back again. He was working overtime now in an effort to increase his wages and he was always hungry. He went down the same street where he thought he had seen Mimi and then widened his search to bars and restaurants. That evening for the first time he saw girls about Mimi's age outside the bars touting for business. Perhaps this was the sort of place where she worked. He couldn't imagine how she could stand it. She had had no experience of such things. In fact she had led more of a sheltered existence than most other girls he knew. He had to find her and take her away before too much damage was done.

Presently he came to a covered open area where several street sleepers had settled down for the night. Trang's attention was taken by a young lad of about twelve squatting on his haunches. He looked like a skeleton hunched up there, utterly dejected.

Then, as he watched, he saw three young men walking towards the boy. They stopped and bent over, talking quietly to him. They laid their hands on his head and shoulders as though encouraging him, and then they helped him to his feet and led him away. They passed right by Trang and one of them looked at him. Trang was struck by the compassion in his eyes. There was something familiar about this man and then he remembered. It was Ah Cheng, the young man who had helped him find somewhere to sleep that first night when he had left Mimi at the hospital. This, thought Trang, is a man I could trust.

That night as he lay down to snatch a few hours sleep he knew that he was never going to find Mimi on his own. There was nothing for it but to go along with Lee Tong. Time was short, and if he was to meet the deadline he must find some way of getting the money. Since Lee Tong knew so much about him, Trang had become suspicious of the foreman at work. Someone must have been passing information about him and there was no one else he could think of. But now he needed his help. At the risk of arousing the man's curiosity he would have to ask for a loan.

Chapter 6

The next day he went to the foreman and asked for a week's wages in advance.

'It's not our policy to advance money,' the fellow said. What's this for?'

'I want it for my sister,' said Trang. 'She hasn't been well. She needs treatment.'

The foreman looked at him with interest. 'She went missing, didn't she? So she's turned up?'

'I know where she is,' Trang hedged. 'I'm going to fetch her.'

'I'm glad she's back. How did you find her?'

The foreman seemed to know nothing about it. Trang decided to question him.

'Do you know a man called Lee Tong?'

The man shook his head. 'Never heard of him. Why should I?'

'Because he seems to know all about me, my name and where I work. He has promised to take me to my sister but not until I pay him.'

'You want to be careful. Where did you meet him?'

'On the water front. He came and spoke to me. I don't know where he got the information from. Either someone told him, or for some reason he's been watching me.'

'Sounds to me as though he belongs to a Triad gang. They make it their business to find out when people are in difficulties so that they can extract money from them. If you'd taken my advice and joined a society they would have left you alone. They don't usually go for people who have the protection of a society.'

'But how did he know me?'

'If they really know your sister, she might have told them where you're working. On the other hand they might be fabricating a story to get money out of you.'

'Mimi doesn't know where I'm working.'

'Then I've no idea.'

Trang looked at the foreman and he thought he was probably speaking the truth.

'Have you been talking to any of the fellows here? This man could have questioned them. You could make enquiries. There are many ways of finding out if someone's looking for you.'

'But why should they?' protested Trang. It was frightening to think that people like Lee Tong knew all about him and could use the information in this way.'

'If they know your sister and she's told them she has no family except you, in other words no-one who would know where to look for her, they would see it as a way of making money out of you both.'

'But that's illegal!'

'Yes. But there's not much the police can do about it. It's happening all the time. It's what's known as a protection racket.'

'Then there's nothing I can do but go along with it?'

'If you want to see your sister.'

'Then please will you let me have the money?'

The foreman shook his head. 'Much though I sympathise and would like to help, there's nothing I can do. The boss would never agree to it. He knows all about loans. Sometimes he gets the money back and sometimes not. Once a man gets into debt it's often a downhill path.'

'I've worked well,' said Trang. 'I've never short-timed you, in fact I often stay after hours to finish a job.'

'That's true but these people will keep on at you and next week you'll be back for more. You could try a money lender.'

'But I don't know any.'

'The fellow outside the factory can be trusted but interest rates are high wherever you go.'

'Thanks,' said Trang, returning to the lathe. He would have to think of something else. He had till tomorrow evening, no longer.

* * * * *

That evening he took the ferry to Lamma Island and made his way to Ah Soon's cottage.

'He's on a fishing expedition,' said his wife. 'He won't be back till tomorrow.'

'Banh?' asked Trang.

'He's somewhere about.'

Trang found him having a meal outside the shack. He was looking cheerful and invited Trang to join him. Trang sat down beside him and wolfed down the fish and rice.

'When did you last eat?' asked Banh.

61

'I've cut down,' said Trang. 'Food costs money. You're looking well, Banh. How are things with you?'

'Couldn't be better,' said Banh. 'I've moved into a room in the village. A good deal more comfortable than this.' He jerked his head in the direction of the shack. 'I'm earning a decent wage now and it's interesting work. Have you found Mimi?'

'I'm about to,' said Trang. He went on to tell Banh all that had happened. 'I've got to have the money by Thursday,' he added, 'or the deal's off. Banh, can you lend it to me? If I don't produce it I shall lose all chance of finding her.'

'Hold on,' said Banh. 'I'll let you have it. Look, Trang, why don't you chuck in this factory job and come and work for Ah Soon. I think he could do with someone like you.'

'I must stay in Hong Kong. Maybe I'll come back here later. I can't tell at the moment. I need this money.'

'How much?'

'One hundred Hong Kong dollars,' said Trang.

'I'll go and get it,' said Banh.

'Trang couldn't believe his ears. He had expected Banh to raise part of it and then he thought he might borrow the rest from Ah Soon, but Banh seemed to have a limitless supply.'

'How did you get all this?' he asked as Banh counted it out.

'Can I trust you?' asked Banh.

'You know you can.'

'You remember that fishing expedition you went

62

on and you suspected Ah Soon might be dealing in something other than fish. Well, you were right. It was heroin. I'm running it for him.'

Trang stared at him appalled. 'Do you know what you're doing? Suppose you're caught?'

'I won't be. I just take it to his contacts. He pays well. If you want to make money Trang, that's what you should be doing too. Do you want me to speak to him about it?'

'No. It's too dangerous. You don't know your way about here. There are a lot of ruthless people involved in drugs and you're crazy if you think you're sharper than them. If you're caught you'll be sent back to Vietnam, if not worse.'

'You're not talking me out of it,' said Banh. 'I'm not taking the stuff myself. I'm just helping Ah Soon and you have to admit you're finding the money useful yourself just now.'

Trang was silent. He would have preferred to turn the loan down but he had no choice. He would never do anything like this himself. He had seen too many young people in his own country whose lives had been ruined, and there were plenty on the streets of Hong Kong. He didn't know how Banh could contemplate getting involved in it but he wasn't in a position to criticise him.

'Thanks, Banh.' he said. 'I'll pay you back but it might not be for a while.'

'You're welcome,' said Banh. 'Think about what I said. It's a better deal than making bicycle parts for fifty dollars a week. 'This is good money and an easy life.'

* * * * *

Trang was waiting when Lee Tong came out of the shadows. This time he was alone.

'You're a determined sort of fellow, aren't you?' he said. 'Any problems?'

'No,' said Trang. He knew by now that Lee Tong demanded the money up front and he handed it over. As before, the Triad counted it and putting it back in its envelope stuffed it into his trouser pocket.

'Come on,' he said. 'We're going over to Kowloon.'

If that was where Mimi was, no wonder he hadn't been able to find her, thought Trang, as he followed Lee Tong onto the crowded ferry. They found a seat on the covered top deck.

The crossing took seven minutes, and then the ferry churned alongside the pier and the passengers jostled down the gang plank. In a few moments they were on Nathan Road, the main street running north through Kowloon.

'I must warn you,' said Lee Tong, striding along, 'don't try to persuade your sister to leave. She's happy where she is and it would be unkind.'

They turned down a side street and then into a warren of alleyways. The stench was terrible here, a mixture of cooking mingled with drains. A sewer spewed its contents onto the street and Trang had to pick his way through the filthy water and rubbish which littered the way.

Presently Lee Tong turned into a bar through a

curtain of wooden beads. Inside, the place was dimly lit and full of smoke. Trang paused at the entrance. There must be some mistake. Surely Mimi couldn't be working here? He'd been wasting his time and they'd been talking about the wrong girl. He wondered if he would be able to get his money back.

Lee Tong sat down at a table and ordered drinks. He beckoned Trang to come and join him. Slowly Trang went over and sat down where he could watch what was going on.

Men lounged at the tables. Most of them were smoking and had a drink in front of them. Some of them were talking to girls. Trang knew what sort of a place this was, a place for prostitutes and call girls.

Disgusted he looked round studying the vacant face of these women. Some were young and might have been quite pretty had it not been for their heavy make-up. Others were older, their faces lined from their experience of life but all of them had the same depraved expression and looked to be without hope.

Then he saw Mimi. He hardly recognised her. Like the others she wore heavy make-up and her usually long sleek hair had been cut short and permed into a frizz. He thought she looked appalling. She was sitting at the back of the room talking to a swarthy man of about thirty but there was no animation in her expression.

Trang got up to go to her, but Lee Tong put a restraining hand on his arm.

'Sit down,' he said. 'She's with a customer. You'll have to wait.'

Trang continued to stare at her. He couldn't believe that this was his sister. How could she have changed so much in such a sort time? Then she turned and looked at him but there was no recognition in her eyes.

'What have you done to her?' Trang demanded.

'What do you expect?' said Lee Tong. 'You weren't born yesterday.'

Somehow he would have to see Mimi alone. He needed time to persuade her. She had been forced into this situation, he was sure. Mimi would never have sunk to this level.

'Did you bring her to this place?' asked Trang, his voice tight with anger.

'She was glad of a job.'

'Did you tell her what kind of job it was?'

'She knew it was a bar. She's settled down well now and gets on with the other girls. It would be foolish to disturb her. It would only make her unhappy.'

'I don't care what you say,' said Trang. 'I'm taking her away from here.'

'That would be very silly. We treat her well. She has a room and her keep and she's allowed to keep a percentage of her earnings. She wouldn't do as well on her own.'

'It's up to her, isn't it?' said Trang. 'If she wants to leave, there's nothing you can do about it.'

'I think you'll find she wants to stay.'

Trang's eyes were smarting with the smoke. He felt nausea rising in his stomach in this close, fetid atmosphere.

'I want to talk to her alone,' he said.

'It's working hours,' said Lee Tong. 'We can't keep the customers waiting. I'll give you five minutes.'

He went over to Mimi's table and spoke to her. She looked in Trang's direction and then she came over to his table and sat down.

'Mimi! What happened? I've been looking for you everywhere.' He searched her face for some response but her eyes were cold and distant. Beneath the heavy make-up, she looked ill. Her face was thin and her eyes had lost their lustre.

After a moment, Lee Tong went over to the bar and left them alone.

'Mimi, don't you know me?'

She nodded. 'Yes, Trang. But things have changed.' Her voice was flat. 'You see I'm working here now.'

'But you must hate this. You can't be happy?'

'I make a living.'

'But it's dreadful,' he insisted. 'Mimi we haven't got long alone. Only five minutes. Can't you see? You're a prisoner? I've come to take you away.'

She shook her head. 'It's too late, Trang. If you take me away now, they'll kill you. They're violent people. Please go and don't come back. Get on with your own life.'

He couldn't believe that she meant it. Had she forgotten the past, their parents, the terrible crossing to reach Hong Kong? But then, perhaps that had been the cause of all this. It had been too much for her and she had lost her reason.

'Mimi!' He tried to gain her attention. 'What would Mother and Father say if they knew you were here? Don't you ever think of them?'

'Mother's dead,' she said without emotion, 'and Father need never know.'

'But this is no place for you. I had to pay Lee Tong to bring me here. If you send me away, I won't have enough money to pay him again. Come with me, Mimi,' he begged.

He saw Lee Tong coming back their table. He made one last effort. 'I'll have to go,' he told her. 'Mimi, please come with me.'

She shook her head.

'You really mean you don't want to?'

'No. I've changed, Trang. You must understand this. I belong here. I can't leave.'

'I can't believe that.' He got up. 'Mimi don't forget that you're my sister. We have no-one in the world now but each other. We must stick together. I need you.'

Was it his imagination or did he see tears in her eyes as she turned away?

'One day I'll be back, I promise,' he said.

Lee Tong stood over him.

'See, you've had your answer. Let it rest there. We don't want to see you here again.'

He waited till Trang reached the door, then he said, 'I've kept my side of the bargain. Just remember my warning.'

Trang was in no doubt that Lee Tong meant what he said. There was nothing more he could do now, but as he walked back to the ferry, he made a mental note of the direction so that he would be able to find the place again.

Chapter 7

If Mimi refused to come with him there was little Trang could do about it. He went over the problem as he helped wheel the bicycles into a godown where they were to be collected and delivered to shops in Kowloon.

It seemed to him that she was a different person and he felt sure that it was Lee Tong's influence. He was certain of one thing though. When she told him that it was too late and that she wanted to stay where she was, she was lying. It was a convincing lie. Short of kidnapping her, he could think of no other way of getting her back and Lee Tong would see to it that he had no chance of doing that. Besides where would he take her?

One evening when he was in the Wanchai area, eating a bowl of noodles, he saw Banh making his way towards the ferry.

'Banh! What are you doing here?'

Banh stopped beside him. 'I've just come back from Kowloon. Had a job to do for Ah Soon over there. I'm on my way back now.'

'Have you eaten?'

'Not yet. I'll join you.' He ordered a bowl of rice and squatted down on the pavement beside Trang.

'Did you get to see Mimi?' asked Banh.

'Yes. It's no good. She wouldn't come with me.'

'You mean she likes it where she is? That's all

right then. What are you worrying about?'

'You don't understand,' said Trang. 'She has completely changed. She hardly recognised me. I'm sure she blames me for not coming to see her when she was in hospital. Let's face it. I abandoned her.'

'It wasn't your fault. Ah Soon wouldn't give you time off.'

'I should have insisted. She was waiting all that time. In the end she gave up and left.'

'You can't blame yourself for that,' said Banh. 'She knew where to find you. Did she ever tell you what happened?'

Trang shook his head. 'No. Lee Tong said he offered her a job and that she accepted it. I don't trust him. It's more likely he forced her to go with him.'

'How could he do that? You can't force someone to work for you if they don't want to.'

'You don't know Lee Tong.'

'But didn't you ask her what happened?'

'Lee Tong only gave me a few minutes alone with her. I spent most of that time trying to persuade her to come with me but she refused.'

'What sort of a place is this anyway?'

'A bar. She's nothing more than a call girl and you can imagine what that has done to her. She didn't even know about call girls when we came here.'

'She does now, though. She had to grow up quickly. If she won't come with you there's nothing you can do about it. Anyway where would you take her?'

Trang shrugged. 'That's the problem. I couldn't

expect her to sleep in the sort of places I do. Derelict godowns and bus stations. I suppose it would have to be Lamma Island though it's not the ideal place with Ah Soon dealing in drugs and nothing but a shack to live in. And now you...' He turned to look at Banh. There was something different about him. He couldn't think what it was... 'You're not on drugs, are you Banh?'

'I've had a go at it,' Banh admitted. 'I met this fellow who persuaded me to give it a try. I shan't make a habit of it, of course.'

'You're crazy,' said Trang. 'Once you start on that, it will get a hold of you.'

'Don't worry. I know what I'm doing.'

It was no good arguing with Banh. Once he made up his mind, nothing would change it.

'So what are you going to do about Mimi?' asked Banh, clearing up the last few grains of rice from his bowl. 'At least she has a roof over her head and a job of sorts, even if you don't approve of it.'

'I can't leave her there. It will destroy her. I'm going back to see her.'

'What will Lee Tong think about that?'

'He won't like it. He once told me that they have a way of dealing with troublesome people and I can imagine it wouldn't be pleasant. Hopefully he might not be there.'

'But he'll get to hear of it.'

'Yes and I might not be able to persuade her but I must go on trying.'

'I'll come with you if you like.' said Banh.

'You will?'

'Yes. Two might be better than one.'

'But it could be dangerous.'

'I'm not scared,' said Banh. 'I'd be interested to see the place. I've got to go over to Kowloon tomorrow evening for Ah Soon. How about then?'

Trang hesitated. He didn't want to risk being with Banh if he was picked up by the police with drugs on him, but on the other hand it was decent of him to offer. It would be a good idea for Mimi to see that they were both concerned for her and Lee Tong might think twice before he tackled the two of them.

'Thanks Banh. I'd be glad if you came. I'll meet you on Kowloon side tomorrow about nine.'

'I've got some packages to deliver for Ah Soon. It's not far from the ferry, then we can go on from there.'

* * * * *

When Trang met Banh the next evening, he thought something was wrong. He seemed to be in a highly nervous state and his hands were shaking uncontrollably. In spite of what he said, he must be really afraid of what he was doing, thought Trang.

They had some difficulty in finding the place although Banh said he had been there before. When at last they found it, Banh looked around to make sure there was no one watching them before checking in his pockets that he had the packets.

'I shan't be a moment,' he said as he disappeared up the steps to a flat above a cafe.

Trang waited for some time and then wandered off

down the street. Better stay away from the place in case someone asked him what he was doing there. He waited for twenty minutes or so. He had just decided that Banh must have thought better of coming with him to the bar, and decided to carry on alone when he appeared. He seemed much calmer.

'Why were you so long?' asked Trang.

'The fellow invited me in. He had to sign a receipt for delivery. Proof that I've handed it over. Ah Soon's very strict about that.'

'You're scared aren't you?'

'Yes,' Banh admitted. 'Dead scared but I need the money.'

'Why don't you find some other way of making a living?'

'It's not easy. You know that. Maybe if I can save some money then I can look round for something else.'

'You'll be no good for anything else once you start taking it yourself.'

Banh threw him a quick look. 'You notice things, don't you?' he said. 'You're right though. A fellow I knew suggested that it might relax me. It did to begin with, but now I need more of it for the same result.'

'And that's what you were doing up there?'

'Yes,' said Banh. 'I can always get a fix there. So what?' he asked, suddenly aggressive. 'It's up to me, isn't it?'

'I don't think so,' said Trang. 'We've known each other a long time, school and all that and I think we should help each other. So it does matter to me.'

74

'I'd rather it didn't,' said Banh. 'I'll come with you now because I said I would but after that what I do is my own business.'

Trang was silent. They were nearing the alleyway which led to the bar and his mind was on Lee Tong. He was wondering what would be the best way to tackle him.

'Are you sure you want to come?' he asked Banh.

'Yes.'

Trang stopped in front of the bar and then parted the beaded curtain and walked in. They sat down at a table and Trang ordered two orange juices. He could ill afford the inflated prices but they had to have some excuse for being there.

Presently one of the girls came and sat down at their table. 'My name is Yuk,' she said. 'Will you buy me a drink?'

'I'm sorry,' said Trang. 'We're not staying. I've come to see my sister.'

'What's her name?'

'Mimi.'

'You want me to tell her you're here?'

'Please. Say it's her brother. Tell her that Banh has come to see her too. We have a message for her.'

'I'll try but I can't promise anything.'

Trang looked round but he could see no sign of Lee Tong. Perhaps this evening luck was with him and he might have Mimi to himself.

When Ah Yuk returned she was alone.

'Very sorry,' she said. 'Your sister doesn't want to come down.'

'Will you take me to see her then?'

Ah Yuk shook her head. 'Very sorry,' she said. 'Your sister told me she does not want to see you. The girls can refuse to see a customer.'

'Look,' said Trang. 'I must speak to her. Please try to persuade her.'

Ah Yuk shook her head but her eyes were sympathetic. 'I try but she won't come.'

'Where's Lee Tong this evening?' asked Trang, thinking that perhaps he was the reason for the refusal.

'He went out,' said Ah Yuk. 'The lady boss is in charge tonight. She not let you see Mimi.'

'Why don't you just go and find her?' asked Banh.

Ah Yuk shook her head. 'No. If Lee Tong come back, terrible trouble for you. Mimi too. You better go.'

Banh was already on his feet. 'Come on, Trang. We're wasting our time. We'd better go.'

Had he been alone, he might have stuck it out but he had to believe Ah Yuk. He might make it worse for Mimi and put Lee Tong on his guard. If he was to get Mimi back perhaps the only way to do it was through Lee Tong but he had no idea how.

'Alright,' he said reluctantly. 'But I'm not giving up. Please tell my sister that I'll be back for her.'

He went outside closely followed by Banh.

'That was a silly thing to say,' said Banh. 'If Lee Tong gets to hear of it he'll take it out on you and Mimi as well.'

'I meant it,' said Trang. 'I want Mimi to know that I won't take no for an answer.'

They had almost reached the end of the alleyway when two men appeared round the corner ahead of them. One was Lee Tong, the other a fellow that Trang hadn't seen before. They stopped in the middle of the alleyway, effectively blocking the entrance. And there they waited. It was too late to take evasive action. Trang walked on towards them with fear in his heart.

'I'm sorry you didn't take my advice seriously,' said Lee Tong. 'What brought you back?'

'You know very well,' said Trang.

'She doesn't want to see you. We don't like our girls bothered by unwelcome customers. And this time I see you've brought a helper?'

'He's a friend of Mimi's,' said Trang. 'Is there a law against visiting my sister? She isn't your property.'

'You're wrong there. She is exactly that. She belongs to me though I'm beginning to think she's more trouble than she's worth. I think the time has come to teach you a lesson.'

Banh needed no warning. He tried to push past the men as Lee Tong gripped Trang's arm and twisted behind his back. He felt a sharp pain as a knee was rammed into his back and he fell to the ground. As he struggled to his feet, he saw that Banh was running back down the alleyway, hotly pursued by Lee Tong's assistant. Trang struggled to his feet and stood facing Lee Tong who towered over him. He stood little chance but he had to defend himself as best he could. He had learnt self defence at school and he managed to ward off some lethal blows to his body when a fist smashed into his face and

77

he went down again. Then began a systematic attack as his whole body was kicked. He tried to protect his head with his hands but Lee Tong had lost his temper and continued the onslaught at the same time pouring foul mouthed abuse at him.

Trang was dimly aware that Banh must have got away for there were two of men here now. They pulled him to his feet and a final blow to his jaw sent him spinning against a wall. As he sank to the ground he lost consciousness.

He came to in the early hours of the morning and he was alone. He put up his hand to the back of his head and felt the wet stickiness of blood. He was aching all over. Slowly he raised himself into a sitting position and was violently sick. He must have lain there in a state of semi consciousness for some time, before he could force himself to his feet.

He couldn't stay here. Lee Tong would find him in the morning and finish him off. Slowly, supporting himself with his hand on the wall, he made his painful way back to the ferry where he collapsed onto a seat.

People were drifting towards the terminal in time to catch the first ferry across to Hong Kong. None of them offered help nor even seemed to notice his condition. There was no sign of Banh. He must have got back last night. He managed to get onto the ferry but on other side of the harbour as he went down the gangway, dizziness overcame him and he had to rest again before making his way towards the factory.

'What happened to you?' asked the foreman.

'I was in a fight,' said Trang.

'You're no use to us like that. You'd better go and see a doctor.'

'If I can't get to work for a few days will you keep my job open for me?' asked Trang.

The foreman was sympathetic. 'I'm sorry Trang but we can't employ people who get involved with Triads. Too many working days are lost. You'll have to look for something else.'

He was too tired to argue any more. He picked up his jacket and left the factory.

He had no money to pay a doctor or indeed to go to a pharmacy. Just now he wished he could die. The pain in his head was excruciating and his empty stomach heaved with nausea. He had a terrible thirst but he was in no condition to search for water.

Outside on the hot pavement he sank to the ground, his head in his hands. People hurried by but no one stopped to ask if they could help.

Chapter 8

Trang found a place at the back of the bus station where he stayed for a long time leaving it only to relieve himself or begging for a cup of water from one of the restaurants. He had lost all count of time. He slept a lot, his mind floating between dreams and reality. Sometimes at night he dreamed that he was once again confronting Lee Tong. It was realistically vivid and he awoke crying out. Other times he thought of Banh. Why hadn't he returned to look for him? There was a time when they stood by each other whatever happened, but no longer. Now heroin had taken control of him, his only concern was where he was going to get the next fix. He was unreliable and now he had reached the point where he was confused and unable to make decisions.

Trang shifted his position on the hard surface. He felt so ill. It was an effort to get to his feet and had he been able to find something to eat he would have been sick. He thought that was probably because he had a fever.

What was the point of this struggle to survive he asked himself. What did the future hold for him in this hostile place? But then there was Mimi. He had to live for her sake. He had given his word to his father.

His thoughts returned to that moonless night when he had walked with his father and brother through the marshes to the place where the fishing boat was hidden. In front of them went his mother and Mimi with some of the women in the party. They had taken just a few possessions with them. There was no room in the boat for more. When they reached the water's edge, a few more came out of the darkness to join them for the journey. One of them was Banh.

As he was about to board the boat, his father said to him 'I'm putting you in charge of the family now, Trang. You are to look after your mother and sister now that I no longer can. Perhaps one day we will be reunited but we can no longer even count on that.'

He had stood on board as the fishing trawler made its silent way down the estuary as the tide carried it towards the open sea. His mother and Mimi had stood beside him as gradually the night closed in on the small party of people standing on the marshes waving them farewell. He had stayed there long after the others had gone below deck, until the darkness hid them from sight.

His thoughts stayed with this memory for a long time. It was more realistic to him than the present. When he tried to face the present he felt so utterly alone. If there was only someone he could talk to who could give him some advice, tell him where he could go for help but in this vast city he had met no one who had time to care. They all had their own problems.

And then he thought of Ah Cheng. He had forgotten about him. If he could find him he felt certain that he would be able to help. But where would he start to look? He no longer had the strength to walk far. His body was black and blue and every time he moved it was like a dagger of pain stabbing him. When he tried to stand up he was overcome with dizziness.

But if he gave up, if he stayed here and made no effort, he would surely die.

It took him a long time to find the place where he had last seen Ah Cheng. He reached there as the street sleepers were arriving, and settling down for the night. Sometimes the police came and moved them on. They didn't want tourists bothered by signs of poverty.

* * * * *

It was dark outside now. Trang was sitting with his back to a shop. He hoped that the police wouldn't come yet, not until he'd found Ah Cheng. He was certain he would come. After the effort to get here, he couldn't believe that it might be a wasted journey.

Then he saw him. He was coming into the arcade with two companions. Trang struggled to his feet and made a supreme effort to reach him.

'Ah Cheng!'

Ah Cheng looked up, puzzled for a moment, then recognition dawned.

'I remember you,' he said. 'You're looking in poor shape. What happened?'

'I got into a fight. Please help me.'

'You'd better come along with me,' said Ah Cheng. 'I know somewhere where we can talk.'

He left his two companions and led the way onto the street. It didn't take him long to see how difficult it was for Trang to walk.

'Here,' he said leading him to a bench. 'You're not fit to walk. Sit down and we'll take a tram.'

As they rattled along the metal tracks, Ah Cheng questioned him.

'Where are you living?'

'Nowhere. Wherever I happen to find myself.'

'So you haven't found a job yet?'

'I found one in a factory and lost it when I got into this fight.'

'When was that?'

'I can't remember,' said Trang. 'A few days ago, I think. I was looking for my sister?'

'Your sister? Is she in Hong Kong too?'

'Yes. We came together...from Vietnam.' He was past caring about keeping his secret. Besides he trusted Ah Cheng. He went on to tell him what had happened to Mimi. It was very brief. He felt too tired to speak much and he kept losing the thread of what he was saying, so that it all came out in the wrong order. Ah Cheng listened without interrupting.

'We get off here,' he said presently. 'Save your breath, Trang. We'll have a chance to talk later.'

Ah Cheng led him along the back streets of Wanchai, then just as Trang felt he couldn't manage another step, they turned into an entrance and up some stairs. Ah Cheng opened the door.

Trang drew back, suddenly afraid. He had developed a dread of confined spaces. Once behind closed doors he felt he might never get out. Ah Cheng noticed his hesitation and drew him gently forward. The room was brilliantly lit and full of young men, talking quietly together. In the background someone was playing a guitar. Tràng relaxed. It seemed to him to be a warm, friendly, safe place.

Two young men came forward to greet him. Ah Cheng told them to take him to a room where he could rest and to bring a bowl of water and bandages. Then inspecting Trang's injuries, he bathed his wounds and gently covered them.

'I don't think there are any permanent injuries. Nothing that a rest and some good food won't put right,' he said with a grin. 'Now for a shower. There's a small room next door with everything you need. I'll get you a change of clothes.'

When he came out Trang felt much refreshed. He looked about him. The room was simply furnished with a couch and a chair and table and on the wall hung a picture of a man with long hair and a beard. His face was full of compassion, rather like Ah Cheng's as he had listened to his story. Trang stared at it for a long time, then went over to the window. It looked down onto a narrow street with washing strung out on bamboo poles. Children were kicking a ball about, their grubby faces alight with excitement.

The door opened and Ah Cheng came in with a bowl of bean curd and rice and a jug of clear, cool water.

'You'll feel better after this,' he told Trang, 'When you've finished you can lie down on that couch and get some sleep. Later on we'll talk and you can tell me what we can do to help you.'

He sat down and waited till Trang had finished, then he drew the curtains and told Trang he would come back in the morning.

'There will be other people about but I don't think they'll keep you awake. I'll tell them to tone down the singing.'

Trang listened to the music for a while. He thought it was rather beautiful. A deep sense of peace came over him and soon he fell asleep.

* * * * *

He was woken next morning by a knock on the door and Ah Cheng came in with a tray on which was vegetable soup, rice and green tea.

'I don't think I should be having this,' said Trang. 'I have no money to pay for it.'

'You don't need money here. We just want to see you well again. Now while you eat, I'll tell you a story.'

Trang had little appetite but drank all the tea. He didn't really want to listen to a story. He wanted to sleep again and then he needed to talk to Ah Cheng about Mimi. He probably knew all about Triads and the best way to approach someone like Lee Tong. But it would be impolite to interrupt so he tried to concentrate on what Ah Cheng was saying.

'About six years ago,' began Ah Cheng, 'I was like you, without friends, and desperately in need of help, but unlike you my trouble was drugs.

'Perhaps I'd better start at the beginning. I was born in Hong Kong. I never knew my father. He left my mother to bring up my sister and myself on her own. We

85

were desperately poor and my mother went out to work, so we were left alone much of the time. I was always looking for excitement, something to relieve the drudgery of day to day existence, and I found what I wanted in petty crime. There were a group of us and we did everything together including experimenting with drugs. Soon I was dependent on them and that was the beginning of the treadmill. Drugs, crime to get money to pay for them, and then prison. So it went on and if there were times when I wanted to do something better with my life, I knew of no way out.'

He paused thoughtfully and Trang waited. He found himself deeply moved as Ah Cheng in his quiet voice spoke frankly of the squalor of his early life. Presently he went on.

'I had really reached rock bottom. I hated myself. Then one day I met up with a fellow who used to go about with us but he'd changed. He'd done well for himself, married with a young family. When I asked him how he'd managed it, he told me about a girl who helped people like me. He brought me to her place and it was here that I learnt about the Lord Jesus and what he could do for me.

'At the time I didn't believe it. I knew only too well that once you'd got into my state, no-one could help. Besides, I was scared. Coming off drugs, cold turkey they call it, was an agonising experience. I'd been through it in prison and it didn't last. I didn't want to be preached at by a lot of good doers. It might be all right for some but not for me.'

He paused and looked at Trang who was giving

him his full attention now. He knew that Ah Cheng wasn't telling him this just to impress him. He really believed it and Trang could see for himself the change in him. He was a confident, happy man now.

Nevertheless he didn't understand why he was telling him all this. It didn't apply to him. He wasn't on drugs. He'd always had a loving family. None of this related to him, but he wanted to hear the end of the story.

'Well,' said Ah Cheng. 'I found out how wrong I could be. I had never met such kindness as I met here. They really cared about me and although it wasn't easy, they got me off drugs once and for all. There was always someone with me in case I changed my mind and wanted to walk out. More important they taught me how to pray, and whenever I had withdrawal symptoms, they prayed with me and the pain went. Just like that. I'm telling you this, Trang, because he can help not only junkies, but people with all kinds of problems.'

'You think he can help me too?' asked Trang.

Ah Cheng nodded. 'I know he can,' he said with conviction.

For the next few days Trang was grateful to rest. He could do nothing for Mimi until he was better. He was amazed by the kindness of these people. They dressed his injuries which were healing nicely, brought him food and encouraged him to rest. Daily he felt his strength returning.

But he couldn't stay here much longer. He would have to think about finding another job and he needed advice about Mimi. He spoke to Ah Cheng about it.

'We must pray about it,' Ah Cheng said.

'But I need advice, not prayer,' protested Trang.

'Jesus is the only one who can help you,' said Ah Cheng. 'It's beyond the rest of us.'

'But who is this Jesus? How can he possibly help me against Lee Tong?'

'He's God's son and although he died and we can no longer see him, he's here with us and can help us.'

'I know about God,' said Trang, 'but I've never heard of his son so how can I pray to him?'

'Let's try it. Let's ask Jesus to help you understand. He'll do that.'

Ah Cheng bent his head and began to pray. He was telling Jesus about him but if he was God's son, he would know about him already, Trang reasoned. Why tell him? But he went along with it and listened as Ah Cheng prayed about Mimi and asked him to show Trang what he should do about her. And gradually he did feel a sense of peace stealing over him. It was becoming a familiar feeling. There was a lot of love and peace among the people here.

'If you're willing to give him all your troubles he will carry them for you,' said Ah Cheng. 'All you have to do is to trust him.'

Trang found it very difficult to understand. He felt that something much more practical was needed to cope with his problems. He didn't think Ah Cheng realised how serious the situation was, nor that this Jesus had the power to cope with someone like Lee Tong.

'Look, Trang. You can't manage by yourself, can you?'

'No.'

'Then do you want help?'

'I want to know how I can get Mimi back. Surely there's some other way?'

'I don't think there is.'

Trang was thoughtful. In his experience you never got anything without working for it.

'Why should I get help when I've done nothing to deserve it?' he asked.

'You're expected to give something in return. Your trust.'

'But God is for good people, people who have done nothing wrong. He wouldn't want anything to do with the dreadful things Mimi is involved with, nothing like that.'

'Wrong again,' said Ah Cheng. 'It's just what Jesus does want to do something about. He came to live on earth so that he could help people who are in those dreadful situations, in deep trouble like Mimi and you. He spent his life with people like that and people far worse. He wasn't nearly so interested in religious people who thought they were quite good enough for him. He spent all his time healing people and bringing them through their difficulties and he still does. But we have to ask him first.'

'How can he when he's dead?'

'When he died it was a terrible death. He was beaten up and nailed to a cross but although he was God's son, he was willing to go through with it so that people who are truly sorry for the sinful things they do, will be forgiven. Jesus paid the price of forgiveness by dying in this way. You see, sin separates us from God but because Jesus died for us, as soon as we ask for forgiveness we can come close to him again. God made this promise and so when Jesus died and came back again in a different form, he could be right here with you and me.'

'I can understand what you're saying,' said Trang, 'but I don't think I can believe it. It's too amazing and I don't think it's going to work for me. How can he possibly cope with someone like Lee Tong? And unless I can believe this, I can't pray about it, can I?'

'You can leave it with us here to pray for you, so long as you agree to it and you want to get to know him. That's a beginning.'

'I shall have to think about it but thank you Ah Cheng. I know you want to help me.'

Ah Cheng didn't try to persuade him. He simply said 'If you ever feel like coming again, Trang, you know where to find us.'

As he went down the stairs and onto the street, he felt bitter disappointment. He had depended on these good people to help him and it just wasn't going to work. They had cared for him. They couldn't have been kinder but they were out of touch when it came to the real problems of life. Kind though they were, they simply didn't understand just how ruthless someone like Lee Tong could be.

Now he would have to think of some other way.

Chapter 9

It was not long before Trang felt that he must make another effort to see Mimi. If only he could make her understand how much he loved her and needed her, he was sure she would eventually agree to leave the bar. If he couldn't manage to persuade her he would lose her for good and she would go steadily downhill. Somehow he had to break Lee Tong's hold on her. He had no illusions about him. He meant what he said and next time he was seen at the bar, he was sure he would try and finish him off.

The next day he went back to Kowloon. As he turned into the narrow alleyway and passed the place where Lee Tong had kicked him unconscious, his steps faltered. He tried to think of Ah Cheng. Perhaps if he had his faith he might be able to return to the bar without this terrible fear gripping him but right now he found no comfort in the thought. He had to stand on his own feet and try as best he could. His parents would expect it of him. He pulled himself together and walked on.

It was mid-day and there were few customers in the bar. A couple of sailors off the British naval ships in harbour and the odd local man. There was no sign of Lee Tong but Ah Yuk had seen him and came over to his table.

'So you have come back?'

'Yes. I've come to see Mimi.'

Ah Yuk shook her head. 'It's no good, Trang. She won't see you.'

'But why not, Ah Yuk?'

'She used to talk about you a lot,' said Ah Yuk. 'Said she must find you sometime.'

'It was I who found her. Now she doesn't seem to want to know me. Why is it?'

Ah Yuk fixed him with a level gaze from her wide brown eyes.

'She's afraid. She's ashamed. She can't face you. Don't be too hard on her.'

'I won't but why doesn't she speak to me? She can't like being here surely?'

'Of course she doesn't but she's past caring.'

'And what about you?' asked Trang. 'How long have you been in this place?'

'Since I was twelve. I have nowhere else to go. My mother sold me as she couldn't afford to keep me. I'm different from Mimi. She came from a good home and she didn't know such places existed.'

'How did she take it?'

Ah Yuk was thoughtful, as though she was weighing up how much to tell him. 'To begin with she was terrified,' she said slowly. 'In a way she was suffering from shock. We had quite a time with her.'

'Did she ever tell you how she came to be here? You see she was in hospital and by the time I went to see her, she had discharged herself. I never knew what happened.'

Ah Yuk nodded. 'She used to talk about it. She was worried because she knew you would try to find her. She wanted to leave but they always kept a close watch on her. She told me she was picked up on the water front. When Lee Tong learned that she was alone he brought her here with the promise of a job. They're always on the look out for young girls because there's money to be made from them.'

'It sounded as though she gave up hope,' said Trang, blaming himself bitterly.

'Do you want me to go on?' asked Ah Yuk.

Trang nodded. He had to hear it all.

'When Lee Tong forced his attention on her,' Ah Yuk continued, 'it was too much for Mimi and she fought against it but Lee Tong was too strong for her. In the end they gave her drugs to calm her down. Now she belongs to the Triads. I'm telling you this,' Ah Yuk said gently, 'so that you will understand why she acts as she does towards you. She's confused.'

Trang felt sickened. He closed his eyes and shuddered to think what degradation she had been through. They had destroyed her, turned her into a creature who would never forget those experiences. His gentle, innocent, fun loving sister! His fists on the table were clenched and white.

Ah Yuk put a hand on his arm. 'Don't take it too badly. She has accepted it now. We all have. This is the life we're expected to lead and there's nothing we can do about it. It's useless to complain. They own us.'

'Who owns you?'

'The Triads. We are owned by one of the biggest societies in Hong Kong but there are others as well. Once you belong to a gang there's no escape, only...'

Trang followed Ah Yuk's gaze. There was fear in her eyes and Trang saw the reason. Lee Tong had come into the bar and stood watching them.

'I must go,' said Ah Yuk, getting hurriedly to her feet.

Lee Tong took her seat opposite Trang.

'So you didn't think I was serious,' he said. 'I must say your persistence puzzles me.'

'I want my sister back,' said Trang.

'There's no chance of that. Your sister is popular with our customers. We wouldn't want her to leave.'

'I'll buy her from you,' said Trang. The offer surprised even himself. He had not thought of this before and now it was said.

Lee Tong's eyes lit up with interest. 'How much can you pay?' he asked.

Trang had no idea what a girl was worth. 'What is she worth to you?' he asked.

Lee Tong named a sum.

Two thousand Hong Kong dollars! It was an impossible price and he had no hope of raising it.

'I'll have it ready for you in two weeks,' Trang said without hesitation. 'But will you give me your word that whether or not Mimi wants to leave, you will let me take her away?'

'I give you my word.'

Trang had to believe him. He had no alternative.

94

In spite of his anxiety he felt an enormous sense of relief. He had drawn a promise from Lee Tong that he would release Mimi. Going back on the ferry, he turned over in his mind how he was going to raise the money. He could, of course, go to a money lender but he had been warned that the interest demanded by them was exorbitant and he was afraid to get into a situation where he would be pressed for repayment. His father had always warned him against it. But then it depended on how desperate you were and if Mimi's life was at stake that could be reason enough.

As the ferry tied up at the quay, he looked up at the Peak. The houses of foreign tycoons stood out white and stark against the green background. Some of the wealthiest people in the world lived there. Two thousand dollars would mean little to them. Yet he could not bring himself to beg.

His thoughts turned to Banh. He hadn't seen him since the night of the fight. He didn't hold it against him for running off. After all Mimi wasn't his problem and when Banh had offered to accompany him, he hadn't undertaken to stand and fight. But he still owed Banh money. Possibly Ah Soon might help. If he was running drugs he would have plenty and Trang still felt that he had some responsibility for Mimi's disappearance. Once again he went back to Lamma Island.

He was shocked by the change in Banh. He found him outside the shack gazing into space. He looked unkept. His clothes were dirty and he had lost a lot of weight.

'Banh! What's up? Aren't you well?'

Banh raised listless eyes to Trang. 'Hullo, Trang.'

'What's the matter with you? Are you sick?'

Banh shook his head. 'I'm Ok. Why?'

'Why aren't you working?'

Banh shrugged. 'He's finished with me. Says I've got to go.'

'But why?'

'He's a hard man. He wasn't satisfied. I stayed too long on a job when he expected me back and he thought I'd gone off with the money.'

'You're on drugs. That's the real trouble, isn't it?'

'So what? It's there for the taking. At least it makes things seem better for a while.'

'You've got to give it up, Banh. It's not too late. If you don't, you'll ruin your life and no-one will give you, a job.'

'I don't want your advice. You're not doing much better than I am by the look of it. Have you got work?'

Trang shook his head. 'No. I've lost my job, too.'

'Well then. We'd better stick together and move over to Hong Kong. We can help each other then.'

'I can't Banh. Now I've found Mimi I've got to get her away from there. I've offered to buy her. I was hoping you could lend me the money.'

'You haven't repaid the last loan,' Banh reminded him. 'How much more do you want?'

'Two thousand Hong Kong dollars.'

Banh let out a low whistle. 'Where are you going to get that sort of money? I haven't got it. I need all I've

got now. I can't even keep up the payments on my room.'
His voice was slurred and he seemed to be losing interest.
'You could ask Ah Soon, but he's a hard man. Very
hard...'

'Where is he?'

'Down with his boats I think.'

Trang got up and wandered off to look for him. The
fisherman was loading lobster pots into the trawler, ready
to be dropped in some rocky cove.

'What's happened to Banh?' Trang asked.

'You can see for yourself. He's useless to me like
that. He must go.'

'He needs help.'

'He has to help himself. I can't do any more for
him. I gave him a good job but he's untrustworthy. I had
to get rid of him.' Ah Soon cleared his throat noisily and
spat. 'Anyway what are you doing here?'

'I've come to tell you that I've found my sister.
She's working in a bar but they won't let her go.'

'Sounds like she's got involved with Triads,' said
Ah Soon.

'They have agreed to sell her to me.'

'How much?' asked Ah Soon.

'Two thousand dollars.'

'If you've come to ask for a loan, I'm sorry. I'm not
made of money.'

'If you could lend me...' began Trang.

'What chance have you of paying me back. Have
you such a good job?'

Trang shook his head. 'Banh tells me that you've

sacked him. If you need someone to do the job, I'm willing to take his place.'

Ah Soon's greedy eyes showed signs of interest. 'Do you know what it entails?'

'I've a pretty good idea.'

'It's running drugs. You understand the risk? It's no good to me if you're going to be picked up by the police and they trace it back to me. It's dangerous but I'll pay you well.'

Trang swallowed, overwhelmed by the enormity of what he was going to do.

'It's got to be on a regular basis, mind,' the fisherman went on. 'It's going to take you a while to learn the job and find new contacts. You've got to find your way around, learn how to steer clear of trouble. I'm not sure...'

'How much will you pay me?' asked Trang.

'I'll give you the money you ask for in advance, then it will be regular payouts on a commission basis. You'll have your cut of the profits.'

'Alright,' said Trang. 'I agree to that.'

Ah Soon took him into a small room which he kept locked at the back of his cottage. It contained a filing cabinet, a table and a couple of chairs. Ah Soon got out a notebook and wrote down some names and addresses which he gave Trang.

'You'll have to learn these off by heart,' he said. 'If you're caught with pieces of paper on you, it would make it dangerous for the dealers. Learn them, and let me have it back.'

He laid a map of the area on the table and explained to Trang where the streets were. Then he described some of the landmarks and named the contacts. Trang listened carefully. It seemed fairly straight forward.

'First you will go to these places by yourself and make yourself known. When you're familiar with the situation I shall want you to take the packets with you and get a receipt for them. Collecting the money won't be your responsibility. I do that myself.'

There were no problems to begin with. Trang located the contacts, introduced himself and arranged the next meeting. But when some nights later, he set out on his first assignment with packets of heroin in a plastic bag, it was a very different matter. He tried to behave as though he was going about his normal business without a care in the world but the light packages weighed heavily in his hand and he felt that eyes were watching him from all sides. He slowed down at the corner of every street and if he saw anyone who might be on the look-end for pushers, he would wait until the coast was clear before continuing on his way.

He was assailed by doubts. Supposing there was no-one to receive the packages? Suppose a policeman was passing just as he was handing them over? Just suppose he was stopped and searched on the ferry? There were always policemen looking for law breakers. He preferred to work during daylight hours when he could mingle with the crowds, but sometimes Ah Soon wanted him to meet up with a contact at night when the streets were empty.

It was at times like these when his job took him through the back streets and past bars and opium dens. He saw again the bodies, more dead than alive, lying on the streets, victims of drugs - and his conscience smote him. If his family knew what he was doing, pushing the substance that would eventually find its way into the hands of these young people and destroy their lives, he could never face them. This surely was what Ah Cheng meant when he spoke of sin.

Then, when his nerve failed him, he thought of Mimi. He had to continue.

He gave a lot of thought as to where he would bring her. It had to be somewhere safe where Lee Tong would be unable to find her. The shack on Lamma island would be quite unsuitable. She needed care and attention, someone to look after her. How could he leave her all day while he was working? She could be picked up again, if not by Lee Tong then by someone like him. The problem seemed insurmountable. Was he doing the right thing? At least now she had food and shelter. If he was to bring her away from there, he must at least provide these essentials if she was ever to recover.

Returning late one evening, he found the last ferry had left for Lamma Island. He went and bought himself something to eat and then looked for shelter on the waterfront. It was beginning to rain and he headed towards a derelict godown he knew of near the docks. He had almost reached it when he noticed a small figure sitting huddled against a building. As he drew closer, he saw by the dim light of a street lamp that it was a boy of about eleven. He seemed oblivious of the rain pelting down.

'Do you need help?' he asked.

The boy looked up at him. 'You can't help me. No-one can.'

He certainly looked without hope. Half starved, his shorts and old pullover in tatters, it was the expression in his eyes which moved Trang. He felt he must do something for this boy who seemed to be in as desperate a situation as himself.

'When did you last eat?' he asked.

'Yesterday,' said the boy. He spoke in such a low voice that Trang had to bend over him to catch it. He squatted down and handed the boy the meat roll and a sweet rice cake he had bought for himself and then he opened a can of orangeade and passed it to him.

'What's your name?' asked Trang, as the boy ate.

'Ming.'

'Where do you live, Ah Ming? Have you no family?'

Ah Ming shook his head. 'My father's in prison and my mother gave up on me. I was always in trouble.'

'School?' asked Trang.

'I left. I joined the Triads. It made sense at the time. I know now that it was a mistake.'

'Tell me about them.'

Ah Ming looked up, surprised. 'Everyone knows about the Triads. Why not you?'

'I haven't been here so long.'

'You'll find out about them soon enough.' The

boy fell silent. He didn't seem to want to talk about it any more.

'I've had some dealings with them myself,' said Trang, hoping that this might encourage Ah Ming to continue. It seemed that a lot of people in this place were involved with Triads, but he had never met an actual member before that he could question. 'And they didn't impress me,' he added.

'You mean you're a member of a gang?' asked the boy. 'You must be a Sai Lo then?'

'What's a Sai Lo?'

'A younger brother. When you first join the Triads you're put in the charge of a more experienced gang member. You learn the ropes from him and you have protection from other gangs in return for what you do for them.'

'Like what?'

'Running errands, selling tickets for filthy films, stealing, fighting other gangs.'

'No, I'm not a member,' said Trang. 'I'm trying to keep out of their way but there seem to be a lot of them about.'

'Thousands. There must be more than fifty different gangs, some more important than others.

'Where do they get their members from?' asked Trang.

'All over the place. Some of them are high officials, right down to those with the lowest paid jobs. They operate everywhere.'

The boy took a long drink. Trang waited to give

him a chance to recover. He was having some difficulty in speaking and his words were interspersed with fits of coughing.

'Why did you say it was a mistake to join them?'

'Because I had to fight and being small I usually got the worst of it. I'd had enough but they won't let you go.'

'But they can't keep you by force.'

The boy looked at Trang as if he knew nothing. 'Oh can't they? They'll find me all right. Sooner or later.'

He had wolfed down the food and now finished off the juice, chucking the empty can on the ground where it rolled to the edge of the quay.

Trang watched it fall into the water. 'Why don't the police round them up?' he asked.

Ah Ming laughed derisively. 'You don't understand. The police know all about them, but they can't do anything about it. They're rich and very powerful. They've been around for years. They call themselves Secret Societies but they're really criminal gangs. They make money in all sorts of illegal ways. Lending money at high interest rates, forcing people to pay for protection against other gangs. They're into everything, anywhere they can make money. They're ruthless.'

It was raining hard now and the overhang of the roof did little to protect them.

'I know where we can get shelter for the night,' said Trang. 'Want to come?'

The boy followed him and Trang led him to a derelict godown which had once been used for storing grain. Parts of it were relatively dry and he found some sacks on which they could lie. He lay awake for a long time wondering how he could help the boy. It wasn't enough to give him some loose change for food and turn him away. He wanted to question him further but Ah Ming was already asleep. He could hear his breathing, a rasping noise in his chest.

By the next morning he had decided what to do.

'I think I know where you could stay for a while, anyway until you're better,' he told him.

Ah Ming looked at him alarmed.

'I'm Okay. Thanks for the food but I can manage now.'

'I'll take you there if you like.'

Ah Ming shook his head. 'I don't want to go to one of those hostel places. You have to go along with the rules.'

'All right,' said Trang. 'I understand how you feel but I'll tell you where it is in case you change your mind. Now listen...'

He had made a careful note of the place where Ah Cheng had taken him and now he described it to Ah Ming. 'You'll find good people there. They'll help you, I'm sure.'

He put his hand in his pocket and brought out some notes. 'Here, take this. Get yourself a meal today.'

Ah Ming grinned at him. 'Thanks,' he said. He slipped the money into the pocket of his shorts and went on his way without a backward glance. Trang watching his springing steps, wondered if he had been telling the truth when he said he wanted to leave his gang. At least he'd done what he could for him.

He caught the boat back to Lamma Island. Each time he set off on another job he thought it might be his last. Sooner or later he was bound to be caught but he had to take the risk for a bit longer. Just until he had enough for Mimi's ransom money. And then he had to find somewhere to take her. Maybe he would have to take the advice he had just given the boy and go back to Ah Cheng, but after his last visit would he agree to help him?

Chapter 10

Banh did not resent Trang taking over his job. He seemed to have lost interest in everything these days. When Trang was away he spent most of his time sleeping or talking to the local folk, but when he was around he was glad of his company and quite content to allow Trang to pay for their food and prepare the meals.

One evening, when Trang had returned from a job he had been doing for Ah Soon, he found Banh waiting for him down by the ferry.

'I went to the Post Office today,' said Banh. 'There's a letter for you.'

Trang ran all the way to the Post Office. It was the long awaited letter from his father. With beating heart he took it outside and sat down under a tree to read it.

'Dear Trang - I was greatly relieved to receive your letter but devastated by the news it contained. Had we known what was going to happen on that journey, we would never have planned it. We can only act as we see best at the time. I am finding it very hard to accept your dear mother's death. She did not want to leave but I felt it best that she should accompany you in the hope that Ky and I would soon be following. The future here is very uncertain. There is little freedom. I hear many boat people are being returned to Vietnam and am glad to hear that you are making a life for yourselves over there.'

Trang paused in his reading. They had expected so much of this place. It hadn't come up to expectations, but once he had Mimi back, he felt sure that Ah Cheng would find somewhere for her to be looked after just until his father and Ky arrived. He returned to the letter.

'I have decided to stay in this country,' he read on. 'Had your mother been with you I would have made every effort to come and we could have been together, but I am too old to face a new life without her. It's different for Ky. I think perhaps one day your brother might follow you. If he does, he knows where to find you. Meanwhile, I know that you and Mimi will care for one another. I shall look forward eagerly to your letters.' It was signed 'Your loving father'.

Trang felt near to tears. He knew now that he would never see his father again. It was more important than ever now that he should rescue Mimi, and to do that he must continue working for Ah Soon.

He watched Banh coming over to join him and handed him the letter. Banh read it slowly, then seeing how upset Trang was, he put a hand on his shoulder.

'Don't worry, Trang. We'll be okay. I know I haven't been much good to you in the past, but I'll try and do better.'

Trang smiled at him, grateful for his effort but he couldn't believe that Banh really meant it.

It took another two weeks before he had earned enough to satisfy Ah Soon. The fisherman paid Trang the money he owed him plus the amount of the loan that

Trang had asked for. He made him sign a receipt together with a promise note that he would continue to work for him till the debt was paid.

Trang had never handled so much money. As Ah Soon finished counting it out in front of him he was reluctant to pick it up. He could so easily lose it. He felt guilty at what he had done and would be forced to continue to do before it was paid off. The thought that it was the only way somehow failed to convince him. Just as soon as it was paid off he would find himself a job with some honest fisherman which would enable him to look after Mimi and lead a simple, decent life. Then he must try and do something about Banh. He felt responsible for him as well.

Ah Soon wrapped the notes in a piece of newspaper and then put them in a plastic bag. Trang thanked him and put the package carefully in his pocket. He wouldn't feel safe until he'd handed it over to Lee Tong, but first he had to go to Wanchai.

He found Ah Cheng writing in the small room where he had slept. Trang put his request bluntly.

'Could I bring my sister here when she comes back?'

'So she has agreed to come with you, has she?' asked Ah Cheng.

'Not yet but Lee Tong has said he will let her go if I pay him enough. I'm going over there now but I have nowhere to bring her. She needs a safe place and people to look after her.'

'How much is Lee Tong asking?'

'Two thousand Hong Kong dollars,' said Trang.

Ah Cheng looked at him steadily. Trang felt uncomfortable.

'Where are you going to find that much money?'

'I already have it. Ah Soon, the fisherman has lent it to me. Will you take her? If you won't, I'm afraid that Lee Tong will try and find her.'

'Very likely,' said Ah Cheng, getting up and walking over to the window. 'Tell me about this loan, Trang. It seems strange to me that Ah Soon has advanced you this large sum of money without some guarantee of repayment. I think this is far beyond what a fisherman earns.' He turned and looked straight at Trang. 'Look Trang, if you want us to help you, we must be honest with each other. What did you have to do to earn this money?'

'Ah Soon paid me for two week's work and made me a further loan, but it wasn't for fishing. I was running drugs for him over to Kowloon and Hong Kong.'

'Dangerous work,' said Ah Cheng. 'You know what could have happened had you been caught?'

'Yes. Prison I expect. I couldn't see any other way. I had to find the money somehow, and I've promised to go on working for him till I've paid it all off. Please will you look after Mimi if I bring her here? I can't pay for her at the moment, but I will one day.'

Ah Cheng's brown eyes were sympathetic.

'We will help you, Trang. but first you must give the money back to Ah Soon.'

Trang gasped. After all the risks he had taken to earn it! How could he?

'I can't do that. I told Lee Tong I'd find the money. If I don't produce it, he won't let her go.'

'Nevertheless you must do it.'

'I can't, Ah Cheng. You don't know Lee Tong. Please don't ask me to do that.'

'But you earned that money illegally and no matter what it's for, it's wrong, and you'll have to put it right before we can pray for help.'

Trang sighed. He didn't want to go through all that again.

'But you don't understand...'

'Yes, I do,' said Ah Cheng. 'I understand very well. Even if you were to pay this money to Lee Tong he might not let you have Mimi back, and then where will you be? You haven't done very well up to now, have you?'

Trang said nothing. He wished he hadn't come. He felt that he was in danger of being persuaded to do as Ah Cheng suggested, and then he would never get Mimi back.

'You see,' said Ah Cheng gently, 'this is beyond us. We can't help you but God can, but you can't bargain with him. You must admit that you can't manage this on your own and you need his help. Can you trust him enough to allow him to guide you with this?'

It was beyond Trang. He was desperate.

'All right. I'll do what you want,' he said.

Ah Cheng told him to wait in the little room while he went to find someone to pray with them about it.

Trang sat there feeling miserable. He wondered if

he could manage to get out of the place without being seen. He could not give up that money. He went to the door and opened it slowly just as Ah Cheng came into the next room with a Chinese lad about Trang's own age.

'We came just in time, didn't we?' said Ah Cheng smiling. 'I know how difficult it is for you when you've never done this before. But I can promise you that if you pray in Jesus' name he will help you get Mimi out of this terrible situation. How he will do it I have no idea but I have seen it happen many times.'

Trang was silent. He was struggling with his thoughts. Somehow he didn't have the nerve any longer to turn his back on Jesus. He had nowhere else to turn. Perhaps if he could go along with him some of the way, Ah Cheng could do the rest...?

He nodded. 'Alright,' he said. 'I'll try.'

Ah Cheng and Poon came either side of him and placed their hands on him. He could feel the love and compassion in their touch and then they began to pray just as though Jesus was right there with them. Trang began to believe that he was.

They said how much Trang needed him and asked him to be with him specially when he went to get Mimi. They prayed for Lee Tong too. Gradually a wonderful sense of peace stole over Trang and he was no longer afraid.

When at last they paused, Trang found himself praying.

'Jesus, I don't know you but I do believe that you will help me. I'm sorry for what I did to get that money.

111

I knew it was wrong when I saw what it did to those people on the streets. Please save them from harm. I won't do it again but please, oh please, help me to get Mimi back.'

When they had finished Ah Cheng came downstairs with him.

'You're no longer on your own now, Trang. Remember that. We'll be waiting for Mimi.'

Not if she comes, thought Trang walking away, but when. He wished he could be as certain.

* * * * *

That evening Trang took the money back to Ah Soon. He found him sitting outside his cottage, smoking a pipe.

'I didn't expect you back yet. You took the day off.'

'I did but I've changed my plans,' said Trang, swallowing hard. He wasn't sure how to tackle this and he was pretty certain that Ah Soon wouldn't be pleased with what he had to say but say it he must.

'I've brought back the money you paid me,' he said. He held out the notes to Ah Soon. 'I can't take it.'

'Can't take it? Why ever not? You were desperate to have it.'

'That was the other day. I've found some people who will help me but I have to give this money back to you first. I can't use it because I earned it illegally by running drugs.'

'Who have you been talking to?' asked Ah Soon, suddenly suspicious. 'You're to keep your mouth shut about what you're doing and who you work for.'

'Someone I can trust,' said Trang. 'If I couldn't I would be in trouble myself.'

'Why this sudden change of heart?'

'I've become a Christian,' said Trang, 'and Christians must try to do the right thing.' He felt a sense of pride as he said it.

Ah Soon cleared his throat and spat. Then he eyed Trang sternly.

'What are you saying? That you won't work for me any more in spite of your promise?'

'I'm sorry but I can't. I needed the money at the time but now I've changed my mind. I can't take it. I'm sorry I've let you down but I can't do something that is destroying people's lives, people like Banh for example.'

Ah Soon frowned. 'Banh!' he said. 'He's useless now. I hope I can trust you, Trang. I've helped you out one way and another and it would be ungrateful if you're thinking of reporting this to the police.'

'I won't do that,' said Trang 'not if you stop dealing in drugs.'

'It was a bad day for me when I picked you up from that island,' complained Ah Soon. 'I wanted to help the three of you but in return you're asking me to give up my livelihood because you happen to have a dose of religion.'

There was some truth in what Ah Soon was saying.

'I'm grateful for your help,' said Trang, 'but we've helped you out as well. It isn't all one sided. I will help you fish but nothing else. The rest is illegal.'

'Have you forgotten that you're here illegally yourself? I could have dropped a word to the police and you would have landed up in a detention camp.'

'You'd have had every right to do that,' said Trang. 'But dealing in drugs is a different matter. It's damaging people's lives.'

'You're asking too much. I don't like making money that way but if I don't supply heroin, someone else will. We're poor people, Trang. There's a lot of competition in the fishing industry and we barely make enough to live on. I shall have to think about it.'

He would have to leave it at that for the time being.

He was about to go when Ah Soon said, 'Just a moment. The other day we brought your boat back. It's not in bad shape. A few repairs needed. What do you want to do with it?'

'You can have it,' said Trang. 'I don't need it.'

Ah Soon opened the packet of money Trang had handed to him and counted out a few notes.

'Take this,' he said. 'That's what the boat's worth to me. I expect you can do with it.'

He certainly could. It would help to cover his immediate needs.

Now he had handed back the money he felt a burden had been lifted from his shoulders but he still had to face Lee Tong. He went down to the harbour to catch a ferry over to Kowloon.

He found Banh there staring out over the water.

'Where are you going?' he asked.

'Over to Kowloon. I want to see Mimi.'

'Can I come with you?' asked Banh.

'Not this time, Banh. I don't know when I'll be back. I'm not working for Ah Soon any longer.'

'That's good news. I'm sick of this place. How about looking for a job in Hong Kong?'

'Later on perhaps. As soon as I decide what to do, I'll let you know.'

'You don't think I'm good for anything now, do you?' asked Banh.

'Banh, remember what you said when we first came here... about making a good life for yourself? How you were going to get a decent job and make a go of it. Remember?'

Banh nodded. 'So I will. Just because I'm going through a bad time at the moment doesn't mean that I can't pull out of it. I will, Trang, I promise.'

'You won't unless you make up your mind to give this up. You might need help and I think I know where you can get it.'

'You're probably right,' said Banh. 'I do need help.'

Trang knew that it wasn't going to be easy and that Banh would probably change his mind again but at least he had to try and help.

'I'm going to Mimi now but I'll be back for you,' he promised. 'Then we'll sort out something together.'

He left Banh sitting disconsolately on the quayside.

Chapter 11

Crossing the harbour to Kowloon, Trang thought about what he was going to say to Lee Tong. The peace and confidence he had found with Ah Cheng had left him and he was bitterly regretting that he had returned the money to Ah Soon. He knew it had been the right thing to do but he thought how ruthless Lee Tong could be. Far from coming away with Mimi, he might never see her again. This could be the end of him as well.

By the time he reached the alleyway he still hadn't made up his mind how to tackle it. He paused for a moment and tried to focus his mind on Ah Cheng. He knew that they would be praying for him but he felt the need of a quick prayer himself.

'I'm scared, God. I don't know how to handle this at all. Please take care of it for me and if I make a mistake please don't let me lose Mimi.'

He felt a bit better after that and continued down the alleyway.

It was late afternoon and a few customers were drifting into the bar. Lee Tong was talking to the proprietress. He had seen Trang come in and invited him to sit down. He asked Ah Yuk to bring them green tea.

'So you came,' he said. 'I can't say I expected you.'

'Why not?'

'You're very determined. I can't figure out why.'

'Because I care about her,' said Trang.

'Lee Tong rolled a cigarette and lit up. 'You'll only lose her in the end. Why don't you forget about her? She's changed, you know, and she won't be happy anywhere else.'

'I don't believe it. I know my sister.'

'We all have sisters. Some good, some bad. This one's bad. She's not worth the effort.'

'She is to me,' said Trang. 'I'm responsible for her.'

Lee Tong looked at him with a curious expression on his face. 'I reckon if I'd had a brother who cared as much about me as you do about your sister, I might have turned out differently.'

'Families are important,' said Trang.

'Up to a point perhaps. Then you have to make your own way. What about yours?'

Trang couldn't see why Lee Tong should suddenly be interested in his family. He had already made it his business to find out quite a lot about them.

'As you seem to know,' said Trang, an edge of sarcasm in his voice, 'my family is in Vietnam. Our mother died coming over here.'

'Ah yes. I'd forgotten. Somewhere to live, have you?' he asked.

'I'm finding somewhere.'

'What are you going to do if she wants to come back?'

Trang was getting impatient with these questions.

Surely Lee Tong wasn't going to try and argue him out of it?

'I'll face that when I have to,' he said. 'Now can I...'

'Look,' said Lee Tong slowly. 'You could do worse than join our Society. It would give you and Mimi protection. If you were one of us we could work together, help each other.'

'No thanks.'

Lee Tong gave him an ugly look. 'People don't often turn us down,' he said.

'Please will you fetch Mimi,' said Trang. 'You know that's what I've come for.'

Lee Tong got up. 'All right,' he said. 'You've brought the money?'

Trang was about to answer when something made him look across the room.

Mimi was coming slowly down the stairs. She looked pale and kept her eyes on the ground. When she reached the bottom step, she hesitated as though wondering what to do next.

In two strides Lee Tong had reached her.

'Go back,' he ordered. 'We're not ready for you yet.'

Indecisive, she looked first at Lee Tong, then at Trang. He could see she wasn't in a fit state to argue with anyone. He went to her and took her hands in his.

'Mimi, it's me, Trang. I've come to take you home.'

She looked at him with a spark of interest in her

eyes. 'To Vietnam?' she asked.

He shook his head. 'No, but I've found a place where you can stay until you're better.'

She nodded, her eyes expressionless. Any interest she had shown at the mention of home, had gone.

Trang turned to Lee Tong. 'I have no money,' he said. 'What I had I earned running drugs. I won't do that any more. I've given it back.'

He felt no fear. He was suddenly confident that this time there would be no trouble. It was out of his hands now and he knew that those people were praying for him.

'You've come with no money?' Lee Tong stared at him with a strange expression in his eyes. Suddenly all the fight seemed to have gone out of him. He looked defeated.

Trang shook his head. 'No.'

'Where will you take her now then?' he asked.

'I'm taking her to some Christians who have promised to look after her.'

Holding Mimi by the hand, he led her past the proprietress. When they reached Ah Yuk, she put her arms round Mimi and embraced her.

'You're with your brother now, Mimi. You're lucky to have someone to care so much about you. I wish I had.'

Mimi murmured something which Trang could not catch. When they reached Lee Tong he made no attempt to stop her. Mimi didn't even glance at him. Trang wondered if she even realised that he was taking her away for good.

At the door he paused and looked back at Lee Tong.

'I'll never forgive you,' he said, 'for what you did to her.'

Lee Tong looked at him for a long moment. Trang couldn't believe that there was something like respect in his eyes. Then he said, 'If you're a Christian, you'll have to forgive me.'

How strange, thought Trang as they walked out of the bar that a Triad should know so much about the Christian faith.

* * * * *

It wasn't until Trang rang the bell of the Women's House in Wanchai that he felt safe. It was hard to believe that Lee Tong had let him take Mimi without handing over a dollar. He could hardly grasp it.

Nothing dramatic had happened. Lee Tong was the same ruthless gangster and Mimi seemed not to care whether she came with him or not. Yet something had enabled him to take Mimi's hand and walk free. He came to the conclusion that it could only be prayer.

Mimi sat beside him on the ferry in a world of her own. When he tried to talk to her, she answered in monosyllables and without interest. He wondered how much damage had been done. Was this the result of drugs or was it to be a permanent condition as a result of all she had suffered?

How would he ever cope with it? They might look after her at the home for a while but he didn't think it would be a permanent situation. He would have to make some other arrangements. He reflected that he had come up against so many problems lately and each time at the last moment, something quite unexpected had happened to solve them. It was as Ah Cheng had said. If that was God's work, then surely he was quite able to make Mimi better. He might even be able to wipe all those terrible experiences from her mind.

When he rang the bell of the house in Wanchai, a woman of about thirty opened the door.

'We've been expecting you,' she said. 'Jackie told me about you. My name is Mandy.'

Trang remembered Ah Cheng speaking of Jackie and how she had helped him and so many others by telling them about Jesus. If only she could do the same for Mimi.

They followed her into a room overlooking the harbour where she brought them cool drinks.

'I've prepared a bed for your sister. She's sharing a room with another girl so she'll have company. I think she's going to be happy here with us.'

'I don't know how to thank you for having her,' said Trang. 'I had nowhere else to bring her.'

'We're glad to do it. I don't think it will take her long to settle down.'

'She's not at all well,' said Trang. 'I don't think she quite understands what's going on. She had a very hard time.'

'I understand. You mustn't worry. The girls will be kind to her. We just have to be patient.'

'I'm afraid she's going to be upset when I leave.

Can I come and see her?'

'Every day if you like.'

'Before I leave, could I have a little time alone with her?'

'Of course.' The woman got up. 'I'll leave you together for a while. Come and see me before you go. I'll be next door.'

Trang sat silently looking at Mimi. She had gone to the window and was looking across the harbour. He still couldn't believe that she was with him.

'You're going to be well looked after here, Mimi. They're very kind people.'

'Yes.' said Mimi. She turned slowly to face him. 'Do I have to go back, Trang?'

'No. Never again. I'll come and see you here every day.'

She nodded. 'I'm so tired. I don't seem to be able to think clearly. Will it always be like that?'

'No,' said Trang. 'It will change but you must be patient. You've been very ill and you need a long rest.'

'Mother and Father...? No, of course. Sometimes I forget what happened to Mother. Did you hear from Father?'

'Yes. Just the other day. He sent his love. Ky might be coming here later on.'

'And Father?'

He couldn't bring himself to tell her yet.

'Maybe. We shall have to wait and see.'

'I want to go back home, Trang. I don't like it here.'

He could make no promises. It was unlikely that they would ever go back but it was a good thing that she was thinking about the family - something for her to hold on to.

'The important thing at the moment is for you to get well again. Then we can plan for the future.'

She accepted this.

Presently he said. 'Mimi, I can't stay here with you because this place is only for women but I'll come to see you every day, starting tomorrow. You'll stay here won't you?'

'Alright.' She looked at him and smiled. It was the first smile he'd had from her for a long time and in it he saw the hope of recovery.

He left her looking out of the window and went to find Mandy.

'You won't leave her alone, will you?' he asked. 'She could be very frightened.'

'I understand that,' she said gently. 'I've seen others like her and gradually they improve. You mustn't worry.'

Trang left with a lighter heart. There were still many problems to be faced but he felt happier than he had since they had arrived in Hong Kong. Now he must go and see Ah Cheng.

Ah Cheng was waiting for him.

'I hear Mimi's back?' he said. 'Sit down and tell me about it.'

Trang recounted all that had happened. 'I shall never be able to thank you enough. I knew you were praying for us. You know,' he went on slowly, 'a strange thing happened when I took Mimi away. I told Lee Tong I would never forgive him for what he had done to her and he said that I would have to forgive him if I was a Christian.'

'That's true,' said Ah Cheng.

'But he's a gangster. What does he know about Christians?'

'Many know about the Lord Jesus and his teaching but not all of us want to follow him. We have to make up our own minds. I'm glad you already have, Trang.'

'It wasn't easy. I must admit that I thought I'd lost Mimi for good once I'd handed that money back. It's going to be even harder to forgive Lee Tong. I'm not at all sure that I can.'

'If we think being a Christian is easy, we're making a big mistake,' said Ah Cheng. 'We find ourselves failing all the time.'

'Even you?' asked Trang.

'Most of all me. I've lost count of how often, but each time we are forgiven and we must try again. That's why we're expected to forgive other people.'

Trang thought about this and found that he could accept it.

'I have so many things I want to pray about now,' he said, 'but I suppose it's greedy to ask for too much?'

Ah Cheng smiled. 'No,' he said. 'God likes us to come to him with all our problems. He wants us to pray for the people we are anxious about. In other words we are connecting them to God, putting them in his care and trusting him to do what is best for them.

Trang was beginning to understand. He found it strangely exciting.

'Can I come and see you again?' he asked. 'I have so many questions.'

'You can make it a regular thing if you like. Wait a moment. I have something for you.'

Ah Cheng reached for a parcel on the table.

'I've been waiting for an opportunity to give you this,' he said.

Trang unwrapped it. Inside was a book with a soft cover and beautiful thin pages.

'It's a Bible,' said Ah Cheng. 'Inside you will find the answer to all your questions. You can take it away. It's yours.'

Trang was speechless. He hadn't had a book of his own since he left Vietnam and he would never part with this one. He would certainly be back, but now he had to go. There was the question of Banh. Once he was sure that Banh was determined to make a fresh start, he would speak to Ah Cheng about him, but until then he intended to stand by him.

OTHER BOOKS AVAILABLE FROM
CHRISTIAN FOCUS PUBLICATIONS

NEVER ALONE
Margaret Smith

Eilidh and Paul, teenage twins are left as orphans after
the death of their mother. Unwanted by their relatives,
they leave the harsh city and travel to a remote Scottish
Island in search of help.

However, even on a small island, secrets are hidden
and the twins and their guardian are at the centre of this
mystery.

ISBN 1 85792 020 1
£2.99   160pp

TRUE GOLD
Cliff Rennie

The huge Olympic stadium was full of cheering spectators. Among them was Jason anxiously scanning his programme. Gordon's race was due to start in just a few minutes. Surely nothing or no-one could stop him going for gold. Then suddenly Jason gasped in horror. Gordon was in deadly danger! But what could he do?

ISBN 1 87167 690 8
£2.99   128pp

THE OUTSIDERS
Margaret Smith

Donna finds herself at logger-heads with Stewart Steele.
He's an incomer to the area and she thinks he's stealing
from her. But Stewart is not taking the blame and there's
another side to him beside his tough image.

ISBN 1 87167 652 5
£2.99   128pp